# THE
# COPYCAT
# KILLERS

## ALSO BY HUGH PENTECOST

# THE COPYCAT KILLERS

An Uncle George Mystery Novel

*Hugh Pentecost*

F
PEN
C.2

*DODD, MEAD & COMPANY*
*NEW YORK*

1 2 3 4 5 6 7 8 9 10

Library of Congress Cataloging in Publication Data

Pentecost, Hugh, 1903–
    The copycat killers.

    I. Title.
PS3531.H442C6   1983        813'.52        83-9070
ISBN 0-396-08183-5

# Part

## ONE

# 1

A horror story broke in the small New England town of Lakeview on a bright October afternoon, the surrounding hills ablaze with the last of the glorious fall colors. A crime was revealed, so bizarre, so ghoulish, that national radio and television took it up and spread the story from one end of the country to the other. While most people were asking the logical questions of *who* and *why*, local people were most interested in the role George Crowder, a well-known figure in the community, had played in discovering the crime. Without Uncle George and his setter dog, Timmy, a brutal murder might have gone undiscovered forever.

George Crowder was a local boy who had made good. He had graduated from high school and the state college with honors, taken his law degree at Harvard, and embarked on a highly successful career. He had become the county attorney, and most people said he would one day occupy the governor's mansion at the state capital. Along the way he had prosecuted a man accused of murder, gotten a conviction. That unhappy man had been duly executed by the state. Then, months later, it was revealed, beyond a shadow of doubt, that the man had been innocent. George Crowder had performed his duty, trying the man on evidence supplied by the State Police. No one thought he was in any way responsible for that miscarriage of justice, but Crowder closed his law office and disappeared from the area and from his friends and beyond the knowledge of his sister, Esther, his only family. Ten years went by and one day Crowder reappeared in town. He was older, grayer, his face more deeply lined. He built himself a small cabin in the hilly woods north of town and lived there alone, with his setter dog, Timmy.

In happier times Crowder had been an expert woodsman. It had been his recreation. His twelve-year-old nephew, Joey Trimble, Esther's son, would tell you that his Uncle George was the best man in town with a gun, with a hunting dog, with a fishing rod, in the whole state—maybe in the whole world! Stories about "my Uncle George" were endless, and it wasn't long before local people referred to the once brilliant lawyer as Uncle George.

Uncle George, the object of Joey Trimble's idolatry, had done what he could to teach his young nephew all that he could about his own specialties. At twelve, young Joey was a crack shot with a rifle or shotgun, and could handle a hunting dog in the field with the best of professionals. This fact, in that bloody October, accounted for George Crowder's being absent from Lakeview for a period of five days. That absence had almost certainly cost a man an agonizing and horrible death not a hundred yards from Uncle George's cabin.

One of the problems in young Joey Trimble's life was that his father, Hector Trimble, the local druggist, had no use for his idol, Uncle George. Hector Trimble might someday be the protagonist in a novel by some writer skilled in handling complex and contradictory personalities. On the plus side, Hector ran a fine drugstore, was an expert and highly professional pharmacist, and had, somehow, managed to persuade Esther Crowder, one of the nicest girls in town, to marry him. He had fathered a fine boy, Joey, though most people thought his mother, Esther, and his Uncle George were mainly responsible for the way the boy had grown and developed. On the negative side, Hector Trimble was a tyrant in his home. Everything was run on an exact time schedule. If Joey was late for a meal he didn't eat; Joey could have no pets because dog or cat hairs might get into someone's prescription. Not unreasonable, perhaps. Hector could never admit being wrong about anything, particularly his feeling that Uncle George was teaching Joey things that would never be useful, like hunting, and fishing, and handling firearms. Instead of Joey reading things that would be useful to him later on, Uncle George had introduced the boy to Conan Doyle's stories about Sherlock Holmes. In that first week in October, Hector lowered the boom on Joey in another way.

There were to be some national hunting-dog trials somewhere in Pennsylvania. Joey had read about it in a magazine he got, and pleaded with Uncle George to enter Timmy, the setter, in the trials. Uncle George, not eager for glory, agreed, provided Joey would handle the dog. Joey was, of course, ecstatic, until the idea was presented to his father. Hector Trimble put his foot down firmly. The trials would keep Joey away from Lakeview for about five days. Three of those days would be school days, and Hector wouldn't hear of his son missing three days of school for anything so trivial as a "dog show." Esther Trimble tried to persuade her husband that Joey, a straight-A student, wouldn't be seriously hurt by missing three days of school, but Hector was adamant.

"There'll be another time," Uncle George said, trying to comfort Joey.

"But Timmy's at his very best now! He'll never be as good again!" the boy said.

Uncle George smiled. "He won't know he's missing anything," he said.

"He's got to have his chance," Joey pleaded, fighting tears. "You've got to take him, Uncle George. You've got to take him and handle him!"

It mattered so much to the boy that Uncle George took off for Pennsylvania in his Jeep, with Timmy sitting on the front seat beside him like a human passenger. At the end of five days in the field, Timmy had won the championship in his group, and Joey nearly exploded with delight when Uncle George phoned him the news from Pennsylvania.

On Monday Uncle George set out for home, some three hundred miles. He and Timmy reached the cabin in Lakeview about three-thirty in the afternoon. That is when this story really begins.

Timmy stood by as Uncle George unloaded the Jeep, waiting for instructions. Uncle George reached down and rubbed the black-and-white setter's head.

"Okay, champ, go play," he said.

The dog ran joyfully up the old logging road into the woods. Uncle George carried his things into the cabin, put on a pot of coffee, filled his pipe from a tin of special tobacco on the shelf. He knew that Joey would come running up to the cabin as soon as school was out. He would have to have a play-by-play account of the whole five days of the trial. When the coffee was done Uncle George filled a mug, went out onto the front step, lit his pipe, and sat looking at the afternoon sun setting ablaze the fall colors on the hills beyond.

Moments later Timmy, the dog, reappeared. He stood, maybe fifty yards away, barking shrilly. Uncle George described what followed to Red Egan, the local sheriff.

"That dog is as close to me as a child would be," Uncle George told the sheriff, who had been a boyhood friend. "That bark wasn't ordinary, Red. There was anxiety in it. I thought at first he had a raccoon up a tree, or something, but it was a different sound. He went a few yards up the trail, barked again. It was almost as if he was beckoning to me."

"Great dog," Red Egan said.

"When I didn't respond he came back a little way, still barking, still urging me to come." Uncle George smiled. "Well, I owed it to him. He'd just won me a championship."

"And you were curious."

"Yeah. So, I followed Timmy up the trail—oh, maybe a hundred yards from the cabin. He had stopped alongside the road, fixed at a point beside a clump of dried grass. There wasn't anything there that I could see. He hadn't treed something, he was looking down at that clump of grass. I walked over beside him and reached over to touch him on the shoulder. He was rigid as a rock. I figured some baby bird had fallen down out of a nest. Nature of the dog to point it out to me. I bent down, moved the grass around, didn't see anything. Then, just as I was raising up I got a whiff of something, like the stench from a broken sewer main. It was almost overpowering. I bent down again, felt in the grass with my hands. Then, God help me, I heard a low moaning sound that seemed to come from the bowels of the earth, from underground. I guess my hand closed, spasmodically, on a clump of grass. That's when I spotted the tube—a piece of plastic tubing sticking up in the grass. That was where the smell came from, that was where the sound came from, through that piece of tubing."

The rest of Uncle George's story was on radio and television all over the country. He'd pulled at that piece of tubing and it had come away, three or four feet long. The foul smell was gone when he got it free, but he was instantly shocked again to hear that distant moaning sound coming from beneath his feet, from right under the spot where he was standing.

"We live in a copycat world," George Crowder told reporters. "Some lunatic in Chicago poisons a few bottles of pain reliever, and people start poisoning drugstore products all over the country. Just vicious hell-raising, no real motive. Well, I stood there, holding that piece of plastic tubing and hearing that ghostly moaning, and I remembered that, about a year ago somewhere in Texas, a kidnap victim had been tied up, buried alive in a box, with a piece of plastic tubing inserted in the lid of the box and reaching above ground so the man in the box could get air. My God, I thought, could this be something like that?"

Uncle George knew that if there was a chance this was a "copycat crime" he didn't have much time, now that he'd pulled the plastic tube up out of the ground. He couldn't just dig up the earth with his bare hands, it would take forever. Ordering Timmy to stay and stand guard, he raced down the path to his cabin and came back with a pick and shovel. Seconds later the point of the pick struck something solid, and then, after some frantic digging, a coffin-shaped box was revealed.

George Crowder was a trained criminal lawyer. Don t touch anything, call the cops. But there was someone alive under the lid of that box. He'd been moaning only minutes ago. With the point of his pick Uncle George ripped at the cover of the box which was nailed tightly shut. It came away, and for a moment Uncle George stood frozen where he was. Inside the box was a man, arms and legs tied with clothesline. A sickening stench came up from the box. The man must have been lying in his own bodily wastes for days! His eyes were closed. He looked emaciated, his skin a parchment gray. There was no sign that he was breathing, yet he had been moaning only minutes ago.

"Don't touch anything, call the cops." To hell with that. Uncle George took out his pocket knife and reached in to cut the ropes. He felt a painful tear at the back of his hand. Copycat! Nails had been driven into the coffin box from the outside so that if the man in the box struggled he would be painfully hurt. Same as in Texas. Copycat!

Uncle George spoke to the silent man, urging him to "hang on." He managed to get his hand under the man's shoulders and, despite the punishing nails, lifted him up. The man's head dropped to one side and a watery vomit drooled out of his blackened lips.

Uncle George got the man out of the box and laid him down on the grass. He put his head down on the man's chest, trying to hear a heartbeat. Nothing. He tried pressing down on the man's chest, trying to start something, and then, despite the filth, tried mouth-to-mouth. Nothing. He stood up, wiping at his mouth with a clean linen handkerchief. The man was dead, yet he had still been alive only a few minutes ago. Uncle George had been only just that much too late.

Not much later the woods above Uncle's George's cabin were alive with people. There was Red Egan, the local sheriff, Captain Jim Purdy of the State Police and a couple of troopers, Dr. Bill Walters, who was not only the town doctor but also the coroner, a half a dozen local men who had come up with Red Egan when the story broke, and a small boy was clinging to Uncle George. Joey Trimble, unaware of anything special, had, as Uncle George knew he would, come up to the cabin to hear the story of Timmy's Pennsylvania triumphs and walked into the middle of a nightmare. The boy was shocked into something close to hysterical tears, which he fought desperately, trying to hide the fact that he was not a man, just a twelve-year-old kid.

As the crowd grew, including young Tom Andrews, editor of the *Lakeview Journal*, the weekly newspaper for the area, one key fact emerged. No one there had ever seen the dead man before. He was not local, not even a casual visitor anyone had ever seen before. It was true, however, that while strangers are normally noticed and remembered in a small town, this time of year was an exception. With the fall colors in their last glory, hundreds and hundreds of "leaf peepers" toured the countryside just to look.

"But why here, so close to George's cabin?" Red Egan wondered.

"Because they knew I was away," Uncle George said, his arm tightly around Joey's shoulders.

"I don't get it," Captain Purdy said. "They bury a man alive and then give him a tube to breath through."

"Torture," Uncle George said, his face looking carved out of rock. "This man was meant to die slowly, painfully, horribly."

"He—he might never have been found if it hadn't been for Timmy," Joey Trimble said, in a small voice.

"That's right, boy," Dr. Walters said. "Now we've got to get his body to the hospital to find out what really killed him. Exposure, a gunshot we haven't discovered because of all these nail wounds, poison?"

Red Egan, the sheriff, gave young Tom Andrews, the editor, a sour look. "When you get this story out on the news wires, Tom, the whole damn world is going to come down on us. We better have some answers before that happens."

Alone with the boy for a moment, Uncle George's arm tightened around Joey's shoulders.

"Sorry you had to go through this, boy," he said.

"How—how could anybody do anything like that to another person?" the boy asked in a small, frightened voice.

"Sick—crazy," Uncle George said. "There was a thing like this in the papers—about a year ago, somewhere in Texas. Someone read it, copied it."

"Oh, my!"

"Your father's going to raise hell about your being here, Joey."

"I know. I came to hear about Timmy, and—and—this."

"Timmy's sort of a hero twice in a week," Uncle George said. "Joey, listen to me."

"Yes?"

"There are going to be shocks like this all the way along your life. There are people, unfortunately, scattered all over the map, out of balance, out of whack. We have to face that from time to time, live with it and through it. Sooner or later we'll find the man or men who did this, lock 'em away. Try not to gossip about it. Try not to get involved. There isn't anything you can do to help, you know. This isn't a detective-story game like the ones we sometimes play."

"I know."

"Go home and get some sleep."

"I saw him, Uncle George. If I go to sleep I might dream—"

"Dream about Timmy," Uncle George said. He gave Joey a little hug. "Get rolling, boy."

Answers of a sort came from the coroner, Dr. Walters, shortly after midnight—a little more than eight hours after George Crowder had found a plastic tube sprouting in the grass.

"Victim is a white male, early twenties, give or take a year or two either way. Cause of death appears to be cardiac arrest; there are no wounds of any kind except for the lacerations caused by the nails driven into the box or coffin from the outside. There is no evidence of poison in the system. The man was badly dehydrated, suggesting he may have been there for several days. People can go without eating for weeks, but they can't last too long without water

11

and adequate air and oxygen. Perhaps I'm romanticizing, but I suspect this poor devil heard the sounds of rescue at hand—the dog, and George Crowder's pick working at the earth above him—and his heart just gave up. He must have struggled against those ropes and the punishing nails for days. He must have been totally exhausted.

"There is no ID of any sort, no wallet, the labels actually cut out of his clothing. There are no birthmarks or scars from any operations or injuries. Nicotine stains on teeth and fingers indicate he had been a heavy smoker, but he was not carrying any tobacco products nor could I find any tobacco dust in his pockets, which suggests he may not have been wearing his own clothes. Sorry not to be helpful, W.W."

Red Egan's prediction had come true. Reporters had begun to stream into town during the evening, and many of them were waiting at the State Police barracks for the coroner's report, eager for an official statement as to the cause of death and a possible identification.

Those with more of a nose for "color" had invaded the woods in the area of George Crowder's cabin in the woods north of town. State Police had roped off the ground around the hole where the dead man's prison had been buried, but dozens of local people in addition to legitimate press people were gawking at the hole, imagining the kind of hell the dead man must have gone through before his strength gave out.

Uncle George wasn't the kind of help Red Egan had hoped he would be. He was crowded into the living room of the Crowder cabin, a bright fire burning, along with half a dozen reporters.

"You can read the woods like a kid handles *McGuffey's Reader*, George," Red said. "Nothing out there to tell us anything?"

"I wasn't looking for anything when I went out there,"

12

Uncle George said. "I thought Timmy was trying to tell me about a raccoon up a tree, or a bird that had fallen out of its nest, or a hurt animal."

"Your dog has a special language for that sort of thing?" a reporter asked.

Uncle George gave the smiling man a steady look. "Yes, he does," he said. "After that, when Timmy pointed out the plastic tube to me and I heard that moaning coming up out of the earth, I had only one thought—to save a life." He glanced at Red. "After that you came up here with an army. Anything there might have been to see was trampled on, driven over."

There was one person present in the cabin that night who bothered George Crowder. It was a local girl, Anne Hopkins. She was just out of college, teaching in the elementary school, but also covering area news for the weekly newspaper in the county. Who visited Mr. and Mrs. so-and-so over the weekend; that sort of thing. "Local" was not quite the right label for Anne. Her parents were the wealthy Lucius Hopkins who'd bought the old Crane place some years back. She'd gone to private schools and Skidmore College. She was, Uncle George had always thought, teaching while she waited for the right man to come along. Admirable not to sit back and do nothing while she waited. She didn't need to work, but she did. But somehow it seemed out of line for her to be involved in a grizzly murder.

"This drawing, Mr. Crowder," she said in a small, almost frightened voice. "Would you say it was an accurate likeness of—of the man?"

What she was holding out was a drawing made by an artist for the State Police. It was already being circulated to police in the area and would, eventually, go out all across the country if the victim wasn't identified.

"It's not exactly the way he looked when I found him,

Anne," Uncle George said. "He had a few days' growth of beard. "He—he was dead. The artist tried to guess what he would look like alive and well."

"So it might not be an exact likeness," the girl said.

"Might not be. It's a guess," Uncle George said.

"But someone who knew him would recognize him from this?" the girl persisted.

"Someone who knew him well might not recognize him from that drawing," Uncle George said. "Someone who knew him just casually might say 'that could be so-and-so.' You know someone well, they have a special look for you this artist couldn't guess at."

A trooper came in from the outside. "The coroner's made his report to the police barracks, if any of you are interested."

There was a general exodus except for Sheriff Egan and the girl. Anne Hopkins sat staring into the fire on the hearth, a strained, almost frightened look on her face.

"Something else bothering you, Anne?" Uncle George asked.

The girl glanced uncertainly at Red Egan.

Uncle George smiled at her. "Red and I are like an old married couple," he told her. "We keep no secrets from each other. You want to tell me what bothers you about that drawing you might as well include Red, because I'll tell him later, anyway."

The girl's obvious anxiety made her seem very vulnerable. Uncle George felt a natural male impulse to help, to be protective.

"You said someone might look at the drawing and say 'that could be so-and-so,' Mr. Crowder. Well, that's what's happened to me. That drawing could be so-and-so."

"Who?" Red Egan asked.

"I—I can't tell you, Mr. Egan, unless—unless I know for

sure. Would it—would it be possible for me to look at the man himself, wherever they have him?"

The two men exchanged a look. "If you saw him and recognized him would you tell us who he is?" Red Egan asked.

She nodded, not speaking.

"Look, Anne, this guy is a pretty ghastly sight," Uncle George said. "God knows what he looks like now that Doc Walters has worked him over. If you think it might be someone you know, why not tell us who, we can check it out and you won't have to go through the ordeal of looking at him."

"If she can identify him it could save the police hours—maybe even days or weeks," Red Egan said.

"If you're prepared to make a formal identification for the police I think you should have someone with you to represent your interests, Anne," Uncle George said. "Your father? The family lawyer if your father isn't available?"

"No!" It was almost a sharp cry from the girl.

Red Egan grinned at Uncle George. "I guess if you went along with her, George, you'd protect her from us villains."

"I can't protect her, even from you, Red, if she won't tell me what it is she wants to hide."

The girl turned to Uncle George with a sort of desperation. "You don't know my father, do you, Mr. Crowder?"

"As well as I want to," Uncle George said. Lucius Hopkins's patronizing attitude toward the local people didn't enchant them. Hopkins was a man who saw his wealth entitling him to get anything he wanted with a snap of his fingers.

"He isn't really my father, you know," the girl said.

"Oh, wow!" Red Egan said.

"It's not a scandal, Mr. Egan. My real father died when I was only a few months old. My mother married Lucius

Hopkins some time later. He adopted me, I took his name. He's the only father I've ever known. But—"

"But what, Anne?" Uncle George asked, after a pause.

"Mr. Hopkins, my father, had been married before—like my mother. He has a son by that marriage. Jerry Hopkins—you may know him, Mr. Crowder."

"By sight." A young man dashing around town in a foreign sports car.

"Jerry is the apple of Dad Hopkins's eye. He can do no wrong. All he has to do to get anything he wants is ask. I—I'm something else again; something Dad Hopkins inherited when he married my mother. I live by different rules than Jerry has to follow." A bitterness had crept into the girl's voice. "Oh, I went to the best schools and college. Dad Hopkins would have looked bad to his friends if he'd given me less than the best education. But it wasn't until I went to Skidmore that I was allowed any freedom at all. My friends had to be approved by my—my father. I—I couldn't buy myself an ice-cream cone without his approval."

"Look, Anne, this is an interesting yarn," Red Egan said, "but I'm in the middle of a murder case. You obviously think you might know the dead man if you saw him. So let's get going."

"If my father knew—" she said, and let it hang there.

"If he knew you were helping the police?" Red Egan asked.

"If he knew I'd deliberately gotten involved."

"You're a reporter for the local newspaper," Uncle George said. "It's perfectly logical for you to attempt to help us identify the dead man."

"Just a gossip reporter—not a reporter," the girl said.

"What *is* the problem?" Uncle George asked. "We don't have forever, Anne."

She drew a deep breath. "A young man I met in college

16

in my senior year. We liked each other. Maybe more than 'liked.' I got permission to bring him home for the weekend—to meet my mother. He came, and he and Dad Hopkins had some kind of a head-on. He was asked to leave, and I was told not to see him again 'or else.'"

"Or else what?" Uncle George asked. "You'd be punished in some fashion?"

"Not me, my young man," Anne said. "Dad Hopkins would see to it that he was destroyed as far as his future was concerned. And Dad Hopkins could and did do it. My young man was kicked out of college. Every time he got a job he was abruptly fired. Lucius Hopkins has that kind of power, Mr. Crowder."

"A first-class bastard," Red Egan said. "I may tell you, Annie, that's not news to me. He's thrown his weight around in this town more than once."

"My young man and I didn't give up," Anne said, "but we had to keep it secret. We couldn't tell my father to drop dead. He could destroy us both. But we saw each other from time to time—in secret. A friend of mine here in town would take calls from my man—she'd tell me and I'd get in touch with him. We had to find a way to survive—together!" Another deep breath. "Last Monday—a week ago—I got a call from him—through my friend. I called back and he told me he thought he had found a way to get Dad Hopkins off our backs. We arranged to meet here in the next town, to discuss what we could do about it. I went to the meeting place we'd arranged but my man never appeared. Nor has he called my friend since then. I—I've tried reaching him, but no luck."

Red Egan's tanned face had taken on a grim set. "You suggesting Hopkins may have—"

"I'd just feel better if I saw the dead man and knew for certain he isn't—isn't my man," the girl said.

"So let's get moving," Red Egan said.

17

It was nearly two in the morning when the girl, Red Egan, and Uncle George arrived at the hospital, each in his own car. People don't like to be left without their own wheels in the country.

A hospital has a kind of eerie feel to it in the early hours of the morning, no visitors visible, corridors dimmer than when the place is "open to the public," the occasional pat-pat of the rubber-soled shoes of nurses or interns. The air is different, invaded by medicinal odors. After hundreds of visits in his lifetime Uncle George never got over the uncomfortable sense that behind closed doors was pain, perhaps mortal agony, and a desperate effort to square accounts with an approaching unknown. He never felt easy in a hospital in these late, dark hours.

On this early-morning tour Uncle George was aware that Anne Hopkins was clutching his arm, sharp little fingernails biting into his wrist. What the girl feared she was going to see had created tensions that were almost unbearable. Red Egan was at the front desk, clearing the way for a viewing of the dead man. Eventually he beckoned to the others and they walked silently down a dim corridor to an elevator which took them down into a basement area.

"You better get hold of yourself, Annie," Red Egan said. "It isn't going to be pretty."

"I'm—I'm all right," the girl said.

Uncle George felt the girl's fingers tighten on his arm. Red Egan opened a door and they walked into a garishly lighted room. A hospital attendant was standing by a sheet-covered body on a bare table.

"The lady may know our subject there," Red told the man.

"Your move, Anne," Uncle George said.

Her fingers let go of his arm. She took a deep, almost choking breath and moved toward the table. The attendant reached out and pulled down the sheet from the dead

*18*

man's head. The girl, standing rigid, looked down. There was a moment of tense silence, and then the girl turned away, shaken by uncontrollable sobs. Uncle George waited a moment and then moved to her and put an arm around her heaving shoulders.

"I'm sorry," he said.

She spun around, tears streaming down her face. "You don't understand, Mr. Crowder! It—it's not him! I—I was just so relieved!"

Uncle George looked over her head at Red Egan. The sheriff was frowning as he came over to stand by them.

"You don't know this man, Annie!" he asked.

"No! No, no!"

"Never saw him before?"

"No!"

Red turned and gestured to the attendant, who covered the dead face with the sheet once more. "Thanks for trying," he said to the girl in a flat voice.

The two men walked out into the parking lot with the girl and watched her get into her car and drive off for home. Red Egan shook his head and reached into his pocket for a cigarette. "I could have sworn, when she looked at him, that she knew him," he said.

"You and I must be tuned into the same computer," Uncle George said. "If those were tears of relief I've never seen grief."

"Why?" Red Egan said. He snapped an old-fashioned kitchen match into flame with his thumbnail and lit his cigarette.

"Something she has to settle with her family before she'll talk?" Uncle George suggested.

"We'll get Lucius Hopkins down here first thing in the morning," Red Egan said. "If that's the boyfriend he didn't like he'll know him by sight. According to Anne the boyfriend spent a weekend here at the Hopkins house."

"Be interesting to see how Hopkins faces it if we're right about the girl," Uncle George said.

Some people can do with less sleep than others. It was after two in the morning, following a day that had included the long drive home from Pennsylvania and the dog trails, the discovery of a gruesome murder just yards from his cabin, when Uncle George got to bed. It was only a little after six in the morning when daylight seeped through the cabin windows and he woke. Four hours and he was as good as new.

George Crowder's cabin in the woods was not without its luxuries. His own electric generator provided him with lights, cooking facilities, heat when the winter cold went beyond the capabilities of his fireplace and his potbellied wood stove, an icebox. It also provided him with hot water for a refreshing shower and shave.

Timmy, the setter dog, was eager for a new day when Uncle George poured himself a cup of coffee from his coffee machine and sat down to a breakfast of juice, ham and eggs, toast and jam. Timmy sat near the door, ears up, eyes bright, almost saying the words "Let's get going." Uncle George was not to be hurried. Looking ahead he guessed this might be the only relaxed meal he'd have for some time. Still, he wanted a little time to himself outside the cabin before cops, reporters, and local curiosity peepers began to descend on him again. It had been a little after four the previous afternoon when Timmy had called his attention to that plastic tube in the grass through which a dying man was sucking his last breaths. By the time he'd uncovered the grave and tried, unsuccessfully, to revive the man in that gruesome box and gone for help, it had been dark. After that a herd of buffalo might have done less damage to any physical evidence around the scene of the murder grave than the scores of people who'd come crowding in from the village. Red Egan had been right. Under normal conditions George Crowder might have been able to put together a story of what had happened from what could be seen along the trail and around the grave site. While there had been daylight by which to see anything Uncle George had been far too busy to play detective. After dark any signs that might have been there had been obliterated by a stampede of people. Still, there might be something above or below the site that had escaped destruction by some miracle. Breakfast finished, the man and his dog went out to look.

The woods were thick, almost from the edge of the highway below the cabin to the top of the green mountain above it. The old logging road, passing only yards from the cabin, climbed to a ridge about a mile above it. Years ago wood had been brought out by a small lumbering company in town. Before the Crowder cabin had been built the company had abandoned its use for a more accessible location on the other side of the mountain. Now the old road was used only to reach the Crowder cabin by the owner and his friends. The upper portion was overgrown, scarcely usable except for a vehicle like a four-wheel-drive Jeep or a tractor. Local hunters and fisherman used it occasionally to reach higher ground on foot, but not often.

Uncle George felt certain of one thing. The man, still alive in his gruesome box, could not have been brought in through the woods on foot. It had to have been driven in on a pickup truck or in the rear of a hatchback car. The people involved had driven in from the highway, past the cabin, and on another hundred yards. They couldn't have gone much farther than the place where they'd buried the box in the dried grass. There was no way to come in from the top of the mountain in the car. There was now really no place to look for anything in the trampled and driven-over road between the highway and the grave. Yet there might be

21

something that had been dropped and bounced off to the side of the logging road. There might be a piece of paper or cloth that had been lost and blown a little away in the night breezes.

Uncle George and his dog walked down the side of the old road toward the highway, searching a few yards off the track all the way down. They planned to come up the other side but they never did, not that morning. When they were a few yards from the highway, little traffic at that early hour on an October morning, there was a screech of tires and Red Egan's pickup truck turned into the logging road. He spotted Uncle George when he'd gone in only a few yards and came to a jolting stop. Timmy, the dog, went over to meet an old friend, tail wagging. Uncle George found himself biting off some sort of wisecrack greeting to his friend. Red Egan's tanned face looked as if it was carved out of stone.

"Captain Purdy wants to talk to us about last night," Red said.

"Probably forever," Uncle George said. "I was looking for something we might have missed, but I suppose the police and the reporters will talk us to death before we can really start doing anything."

"Purdy wants to talk about the girl," Red said.

"Anne Hopkins?"

"She's dead, George."

Uncle George felt, suddenly, as though his feet had taken root in the earth. For a moment he couldn't move backward or forward.

"*Dead?*" he heard himself ask.

"Crazy kind of an accident," Red said. "Little after two when we watched her drive off from the hospital, right? No more than a mile to the Hopkins place. Seems when she got home she decided she wanted to take a dip in the pool. Took off her clothes in the bathhouse there. Didn't turn on

22

the pool lights. Probably didn't want to disturb the family. Also, she was stark naked."

"Drowned?"

Red Egan shook his head. "She evidently ran out onto the diving board and dove into the pool. Problem—there wasn't any water in the pool."

"For God's sake!"

"Smashed in her skull like a rotten pumpkin. Seems Jake Wilson, works the grounds for the Hopkins, had drained the pool the night before to clean out the last of the leaves. When he got there this morning he turned on the water to refill it, waited a while, went from the pump house to make sure everything was working, and there was Annie's body floating in the first of the fresh water."

Uncle George was fingering the tan parka he was wearing. "You know how cold it was last night, Red?" he asked.

"Chilly, I remember."

"Around forty—high thirties." Uncle George's mouth tightened. "Not an ideal temperature for skinny-dipping."

It was a matter of routine that Red Egan, the sheriff, was one of the first people to hear of Anne Hopkins's tragic accident. The Hopkins family had called the State Police when the girl's body was found by Jake Wilson, the "outside man." The girl's body was taken to the hospital where someone remembered that she'd been there in the early hours of the morning with Red and Uncle George Crowder to view the remains of the murder victim found in the box. As a so-called "member of the press" she'd been entitled to look at the dead man, the captain supposed, but why at two in the morning? The body had been available for identification much earlier in the evening. Captain Purdy called Red Egan to ask, and was told the girl thought the dead man might possibly be someone she knew.

"It turned out not to be," Red Egan told the trooper

23

captain, "but—well, there was something kind of odd about it."

"Appreciate it if you and George Crowder could come over here and tell me about it," Captain Purdy said. "We're snowed under here with people who think they may know something about the man in the box."

Uncle George sent a disappointed dog up the trail to "stand guard" at the cabin and rode to the barracks with Red Egan in his pickup. On the way Red Egan asked a question.

"You still think like you did last night, George?" he asked. "You still think Anne Hopkins did know who that dead guy is?"

"Hunch—instinct for the truth," Uncle George said. "My well-known and infallible instinct for the truth!"

"I'd go with it," Red Egan said.

"You're forgetting, my friend, that fifteen years ago an innocent man went to the gas chamber because of my infallible instinct for the truth."

"That's crazy," Red said. "You prosecuted on evidence supplied by the State Police. You just did your job."

"But between you and me, Red, my instinct for the truth convinced me that poor bastard was guilty. I don't trust it anymore, Red. I don't always trust evidence these days. It can lie to you."

"You said it yourself, George. When the girl was crying those didn't look like tears of relief."

"Do I know how an up-tight girl reacts to such a moment?"

"I trust your reactions more than most people's," Red said.

"I advise against it," Uncle George said, that bitterness still in his voice. "I obviously don't know how an up-tight girl reacts, which is why I can't imagine how relief could drive her to take a stark-naked dive into a swimming pool at two in the morning with the temperature down toward freezing. But she did, so I don't score high on how an uptight girl shows her relief."

Captain Purdy, in his office at the State Police barracks, looked glad to see a couple of people he knew and trusted.

"The whole damn countryside wants to have a look at the dead man," he said. "All of 'em have some reason to think they might know who he is. Ghouls, the whole lot of 'em." He gestured to chairs that flanked his desk. "Annie Hopkins got you two to take her to the hospital to have a look?"

Red Egan told Purdy the story—the young man Anne Hopkins had met in college, his visit to the Hopkins place here in Lakeview, the young man's falling out with Lucius Hopkins, the apparent war between them.

"According to Anne her father hounded this guy, got him kicked out of jobs, drove the two young people to communicate and meet in secret. Someone here in Lakeview acted as a message-taker for Anne—took phone calls from this guy. He was supposed to come here last Tuesday. Said he had something he hoped would get Lucius Hopkins off his back. He never came, never sent any message to explain, couldn't be reached wherever he lives when Anne tried. So—she thought there was a chance this guy in the box could be her guy."

"She saw him?"

"Yes. No cigar, she said. Not him. But she cried like her heart would break. George and I both wondered—" Red shrugged and let it rest there.

"So she was so relieved," Uncle George said, in that flat, hard voice, "she went home, took off her clothes, and with the temperature near freezing decided to go for a nice, relaxing dip in the pool."

"What are you suggesting, George?" Captain Purdy asked.

"I told Red, I'm suggesting I don't really know how

young girls show off relief. Tears and an ice-cold swim? New generation. Who knows, maybe that's normal."

"Well, if the guy in the box isn't her guy, then you can take that up with a psychiatrist, George. But if it *was* her guy—"

"Lucius Hopkins can tell you that, or Mrs. Hopkins," Red said.

"It's not an ideal time to ask them to go through that," Captain Purdy said. "But if this man came to their house for a weekend some one of the servants would know him by sight, maybe even Jake Wilson. You know when that visit took place?"

Red and Uncle George exchanged looks. They couldn't remember Anne's saying just when. She'd met her man during her senior year in college, brought him home, and ever since then Lucius Hopkins had been hounding him.

"Could have been a year, year and a half ago," Uncle George said.

"Anne said her father got her guy kicked out of several jobs. It must have been at least that long ago that he was here. Anne graduated from college a year ago last spring, got a job on the paper, and this fall started teaching in the school. That's a year and a half." Red reached for a cigarette. "Could have been before that when the guy visited here."

"You didn't ask her who the person was who was taking phone calls for her?" the captain asked.

"She wasn't prepared to talk at all before she had a look at the body. Afterwards—when she'd told us it wasn't him—there didn't seem any point in asking her just then," Red said.

"But you two thought she wasn't telling you the truth when she'd seen the remains?" Purdy asked.

"It occurred to us that she was lying," Red said.

"Why would she?"

"Afraid of her father," Red suggested. "Or afraid he might have had something to do with the killing; wanted to be sure before she talked; or wanted to get even herself."

"Or, knew she could do nothing, went home, took off her clothes, and dove into a pool she knew was empty, head first onto the cement bottom," Uncle George said.

"Suicide?"

"I have to tell you," Uncle George said, "that nothing lights up in me when I suggest it."

"So what else, then?"

Uncle George's eyes were cold as two newly minted dimes. "So she confronted her father and he killed her," he said.

"My God, George, that's pretty far out," Purdy said.

"You asked for a guess," Uncle George said.

"Does something light up in you when you suggest that?" Purdy asked.

"We don't have any facts," Uncle George said. "We know that man didn't nail himself in a box and bury himself up on the logging road. As far as the girl is concerned, Red and I both think the man she saw in that hospital morgue was her man. Something lights up when I say that. So we have two people deeply in love, one of them grotesquely and brutally murdered, the other one dead—maybe an accident, maybe a suicide, maybe another murder. Those two dead young people have no one to fight for their cause."

"You don't trust us to come up with answers?" Purdy asked.

"I trust you to try," Uncle George said.

"But you're electing yourself to work alone?" Purdy asked. He wasn't pleased. "Red could swear you in as a deputy."

"If I work officially with you or Red I have to play by your rules," Uncle George said. "Official warnings—'anything you say may be used against you,' go no place without a

27

search warrant. We're dealing with some kind of monsters, Captain, and I choose to make my own rules." He drew a deep breath. "I heard that poor bastard crying for help with his last breath from the ground under my feet and I failed him. I think I heard that girl crying for help and I failed her. I owe them both!"

"Don't hold out on us, George," Red Egan said.

"If I find something that'll stick, you'll get it," Uncle George said.

_____ 2 _____ It was time for facts, Uncle George told himself, not hunches or "infallible instincts." It could be pure coincidence that the village of Lakeview had been subjected to two violent deaths within a space of ten hours. There wasn't anything yet but hunch—on the part of two men—to suggest there was any connection between the brutal and sadistic murder of the man in the box, and what could certainly be a tragic accident in the death of Anne Hopkins. Yet if Anne Hopkins *had* recognized the man in the hospital morgue, the picture began to take on an entirely different aspect.

"You get to speculating about wild possibilities," Uncle George said to his friend the sheriff, as Red Egan drove him from the barracks back to his cabin. "Why did they choose the old logging road that goes past my cabin to bury their man alive?"

"Looking for a safe place, saw the old logging road—" Red suggested.

"Or knew I was gone to Pennsylvania for a few days and they could come and go without any danger of being noticed."

"Come and go?"

"They kept him alive with the tube, didn't they?" Uncle George asked. "Maybe they wanted something from him. Maybe they went back to bargain with him, or just to listen to him die!"

"You suggesting they hung around town after they buried him?"

Uncle George glanced at his friend. "You suggest they were just passing through town?"

"Why not?"

"If we were right about Anne—if she *did* recognize the body in the hospital morgue—then they weren't just passing through, and we have to wonder what really happened to her."

Red Egan slowed his truck to make the turn into the old logging road. "God, George, you're saying this killer—or killers—belong here in Lakeview! In our town!"

"Could be your next-door neighbor," Uncle George said.

"Oh, brother! Where do we go from here?"

"So we stop inventing melodramas. We've got to identify that dead man," Uncle George said. "There must be half a dozen people who can tell us if the dead man was Anne Hopkins's guy. If he was, and Anne's story was true, then Lucius Hopkins can tell us his name, where he was last working, maybe what he had for breakfast last Monday before he disappeared from Anne's world."

"Maybe Hopkins wouldn't choose to tell us," Red said.

"Which is why I'd like to get the answer from somewhere else. Mrs. Hopkins? Servants working in the house when Anne's guy came here for a weekend? The person Anne was using as a message service here in town?"

"We can force Hopkins and Mrs. Hopkins to go to the hospital to look at the dead man," Red Egan said.

"They have a dead daughter on their hands whose body's hardly cold yet," Uncle George said. "If Hopkins is a villain in this scenario he'll answer you whatever way suits him. I'd like to find out some other way and then confront him with it. No way then for him to fake you out."

"You're saying Lucius Hopkins is in on two murders?" Red said. "Maybe you ought to be writing for the movies, George."

The tight set to Uncle George's mouth relaxed for an instant, and he smiled at his friend. "Maybe I'd write a tighter script than most of the junk we see coming out of Hollywood these days." The truck bounced up the logging road toward the cabin. "The servants who were working in the Hopkins house when Anne brought her guy there to visit may be our best bet. Any of them local, do you know?"

"A year and a half ago? I'd have to check with Jake Wilson."

"You do that. Find one who was working there when Anne brought her guy for a visit, take him or her to the hospital. If the dead man is that guy, then we've got Hopkins over a barrel."

"And you?"

Uncle George smiled again. "I've got to work on my script a little more, and then just mosey around, see what I can see, hear what I can hear."

Esther Trimble, Uncle George's younger sister, was a strikingly handsome woman in her late thirties. Big-boned like her brother, she had coppery red hair, bright blue eyes, and a wide generous mouth and smile. Looking at her, George Crowder thought his sister was the prototype of the sturdy frontier woman of a hundred and fifty years ago, heading west in a covered wagon. How Hector Trimble had ever managed to corral so much vitality was hard to imagine.

"A horrible experience for you, George," she said.

Uncle George was sitting in her kitchen, a mug of fresh

hot coffee on the table beside him. "I stopped by because I was worried about Joey," he said. "I thought you might have kept him out of school today. He'll be the target for a million questions."

"You know Hector," Esther said.

"Yes, God help me, I know Hector."

"I thought Joey might stay out of school for a day, but Hector said no." Esther shook her head as though her husband's decisions would never stop surprising her. "Hector said that one day of school would be wrecked whenever he went back, so he might better go back today when he was all stirred up anyway."

"Some logic in that, Es," Uncle George said.

"There's always *some* logic in Hector's decisions," Esther said. "And the heat may be a little off Joey this morning. The school will be in a turmoil over this dreadful accident to Anne Hopkins."

"If it was an accident," Uncle George said, sipping his coffee.

Esther Trimble was rarely surprised by anything her brother might have to say. "What do you mean 'if'?" she asked.

"It could have been suicide, it could have been murder," Uncle George said.

"Of course," Esther said, casually. "And she could have been sleepwalking and fallen out of an upstairs window."

Uncle George smiled at her. "You're willing to admit that things aren't always the way they look?"

"I know you well enough, George, to know you wouldn't be running down side streets looking for trouble when you already have a horrible murder within spitting distance of where you live. You must see some connection between the two things."

"Go to the head of the class, Es," Uncle George said. "This is between us until it becomes generally known." He

31

told her about Anne Hopkins, her problems with her unknown young man, her visit to the hospital to view the body. "She said he wasn't her man, but she was obviously in shock, hysterical weeping. Both Red and I thought she was lying to us."

"Why would she?"

Uncle George shrugged. "Wanted to be sure she wasn't pointing at the wrong person, perhaps. Even though she didn't love her stepfather, accusing him of such a horrible crime might be too much. She could wreck her mother's life. She wanted to be sure before she pointed to him."

"She didn't think she'd be in danger, holding off?"

"If she did she was willing to risk it."

Esther reached for the coffee pot on the stove. "And it could be just the way they're saying it was. She left you and Red and went home. She wanted to clear her head for some unemotional thinking, decided a plunge in the cold pool might level her off. Didn't know the pool had been drained, didn't turn on the pool lights because she didn't want to disturb the rest of the household. Went through a familiar routine—out onto the diving board and a springing dive down onto the cement bottom of the pool. It could be that way."

"It could be," Uncle George said.

"But you don't think it was that way. Why, George?"

He brought his coffee mug down so hard on the kitchen table that coffee splashed out onto the oilcloth cover. "Some kind of a hunch that won't go away," he said.

"Most of your hunches are pretty sound," Esther said. Then, after a moment, "You know I'm on the school board for the elementary school, George. We hired Anne Hopkins to teach the fourth grade this fall. Her educational records were good, but the Hopkinses aren't popular in town, you know. Lucius Hopkins carries his nose a little too high in the air. Anne was his flesh and blood, we thought—I thought—until you just told me. It was Marilyn Stroud who turned the tide for Anne."

"The assistant principal?"

"I guess that's her title," Esther said. "Marilyn's my age, we went to school together, she's local—like me. For her to make a pitch for someone like Anne counted—a local supporting an invader."

Uncle George's smile was wry. "Old prejudices never die," he said.

"Not only were Anne's educational credentials adequate, but Marilyn went overboard for Anne as a human being. It turned the tide. I'm telling you this, George, because Marilyn might be able to tell you who was taking and sending messages between Anne and her young man."

"Could be Marilyn herself?"

"I didn't say that."

The door that connected the kitchen to the adjoining drugstore opened and Hector Trimble made an entrance. Hector was tall, stooped, balding, with cold gray eyes protected by steel-rimmed glasses. His skin was pale. Uncle George guessed he hadn't exposed himself to the sun for years, and if he had he'd have burned a lobster red.

"I saw your Jeep out front, George," Hector said.

"I cannot tell a lie, Hector," Uncle George said. "I'm here."

"I just wanted to tell you I think you could have shown a little more consideration to Esther and me than to let Joey in on that horror last night." Hector's voice was tight, high-pitched.

Uncle George glanced at his handsome sister. How on earth, he thought. "I didn't exactly 'let him in on it,' Hector," he said. "Timmy took me to where the man was buried. I got tools to dig him up, tried to revive him when I got him free, went for help. Half the town turned up and suddenly Joey was there."

"You knew he'd be coming to see you—about the dog," Hector said.

"If a man was dying on the floor of your drugstore, Hector, and you were trying to revive him, would you worry if Joey happened to walk in on you?"

"I'd have ordered him out," Hector said. "You let him stay there to see the whole bloody mess."

"I suppose I could have told him to go home, but I didn't," Uncle George said. "He needed comfort, not orders."

"You're not good for that boy, George. I guess there's no point in reminding you and Esther that that's how I feel about it."

"You never let us forget, Hector," Esther said. "It's a point on which we disagree."

Hector gave his wife an angry look, turned, and went back into the drugstore.

That Tuesday might just as well have been declared a school holiday, as far as education was concerned. A double horror had hit the peaceful village of Lakeview and nobody was interested in or talking about anything else.

"Including the teachers," Marilyn Stroud told George Crowder, who had made his way through an army of curious kids to the assistant principal's modest office. "But what a ghastly thing for you, George. Joey says it was your dog, Timmy, who really found him. They think he's been there four or five days. Everyone is asking questions."

Uncle George smiled at her. "Including the assistant principal," he said.

"Oh, George!"

Marilyn was a pretty woman; not handsome, like Esther, but pretty and very bright and attractive, Uncle George thought. He'd known her when Esther first brought her

34

home to the Crowder place from kindergarten, and she and George, ten years older, had been on a first-name basis all those years.

"I really didn't come here to talk about the man in the box," Uncle George said. "I've got Anne Hopkins on my mind. Did you know I was with her only about an hour before she must have died?"

"It's just not believable," Marilyn said, her voice suddenly unsteady. "Yesterday she was here, alive, laughing, a wonderfully inspirational teacher. This morning she's dead!"

"We seemed to have crammed a lot of hell into twenty-four hours in our little town," Uncle George said.

"You say you were with her just before she died, George? Imagine diving into that pool in the dark without even checking—"

"If that's what happened," Uncle George said.

"What are you saying?"

"I'm saying, if that's what happened. Red Egan and I took her to the hospital about two in the morning. She thought the man in the box might have been someone she knew and cared for."

Marilyn Stroud leaned forward. "And was he?"

"She said not, but neither Red nor I believed her. Not too long after that she was dead. I came here, Marilyn, to ask you for her young man's name, his address, his telephone number."

"I—I don't understand."

"Please, Marilyn. I'm not working for the police. Anything you tell me will be a secret—at least your involvement in it will be a secret."

"I just don't—"

"Please, Marilyn. I almost saved that man in the box, but I failed. I think Anne was on the verge of asking me for

35

help, but I failed her, too. I don't choose to let anyone sweep what's happened under the rug. You were Anne's friend, her sponsor, I suggest her confidant. Just give me the man's name, his address and telephone number, and I'll check it out from the other end."

"But—"

"If he wasn't the man in the box he'll be hearing about Anne on the radio or TV and he'll be in touch. If he wasn't the man in the box, then I'm off into the wild blue yonder. I don't want to wait forever to find out which way it is."

Marilyn took a deep, shuddering breath. "I don't know anyone else I'd trust with this, George," she said. "You've guessed right about me. I—I was helping Anne. It had to be a secret or Lucius Hopkins would have had my scalp. The man's name is Paul Comargo. His telephone number is in New York—Manhattan. Area code 212—here, I'll write it down for you." She scribbled a number on a piece of paper and handed it to Uncle George.

"Address?" he asked.

"I've never had an address. I would call him for Anne and ask him to be ready for a call from her at a certain time. Or he would call me and ask me to tell Anne to call him at a certain time. If they wrote each other it never passed through me."

"What do you know about Paul Comargo?"

"He was about to get a degree in computer techniques, communications, I'm not quite sure. He came here, had a run-in with Lucius Hopkins, was kicked out of school—and out of jobs after that."

"Hopkins the villain?"

"Anne said so."

"Why?"

"I don't think she knew, or if she did she never told me," Marilyn said.

36

Uncle George put the slip of paper down on her desk. "Try him now," he said.

Marilyn dialed the number and waited. No answer.

"Who would know him by sight?" Uncle George asked when she put down the phone.

"Hopkins, of course. Mrs. Hopkins. He was a guest in their house for at least one night. The servants were there at the time."

"When was that visit?"

"I can't give you a date, George. It—it was more than a year and a half ago. I've been in cahoots with Anne for about a year and a half."

Uncle George Stood up. "Keep trying him, Marilyn. I'll get back to you." He put the slip of paper with the telephone number on it in his pocket.

"George, if Lucius Hopkins finds out I've been—"

"He doesn't have to know," Uncle George said. "I'll check it out on the other end. No one has to know where I got a lead."

"You think Anne may not—that it wasn't an accident?"

"I think it's entirely possible," Uncle George said.

"Oh, my God, George!"

Lieutenant Mark Kreevich of Manhattan Homicide was an old friend of George Crowder's. They had both gone to Harvard Law School together, one to go into the practice of law and a personal disaster, the other into criminal investigation in the world's most complex city.

From a pay phone booth in the lobby of the school Uncle George called his old friend at police headquarters in New York. Luck was with him this time.

"George, you old scoundrel!" Kreevich said. "You've been making headlines down here. I can't figure out whether you or your dog got top billing."

"It's a mess," Uncle George said.

"Is it true they drove nails in the box so that poor bastard couldn't move without ripping himself up?"

"Remember a case in Texas about a year ago? Same thing."

"What can I do for you, friend?"

"I've got a name and a telephone number in your town, no address," Uncle George said. "Paul Comargo. He just may be our man." He gave Kreevich the phone number. "He may be alive and well and we'll start over. If he isn't and he hasn't been seen for a week, maybe you can find someone who would come up here and look at him."

"I'd love to have a hand in nailing anyone responsible for that kind of thing," Kreevich said. "Can I call you, or will you call me back in a couple of hours?"

"I'll call," Uncle George said.

Red Egan's life was centered around a little store in the middle of the village. He sold blue jeans, sports shirts and coats, winter parkas, pipes and tobacco supplies. In a back room was a pool table, reserved for Red's special friends, and in a corner of that room was the sheriff's desk and a couple of metal filing cabinets. Red was there at his desk, talking to Jake Wilson, the Hopkinses' "outside man," when Uncle George put in an appearance. Jake was a gray-haired, muscular man who was said to be able to make flowers grow in a rock pile.

"Jake's come up with an interesting piece of information," Red told Uncle George.

"Red was asking me about some beau of Anne's who visited out at the Hopkinses a year and a half ago," Wilson said. "I've only been working out there about fifteen months so I wouldn't know. But there isn't anyone else out there except the Mister and Missus and young Jerry who would either. The whole staff was fired, or let go, a couple of months before my time—cook, housemaids, laundress, a sort of houseman and butler. All gone."

"Where are they now?"

"They all came from out of town," Wilson said, "and they all went out of town when they left. I'm the only local guy who's ever worked out there since Hopkins bought the place five years ago. Hopkins had a place somewhere in South Carolina and he brought help up for the first summers he was here. Then, when they moved in permanently year-round, they imported a staff. Story was Hopkins didn't want local people who'd be gossiping about what went on up there."

"What do you mean 'what went on'?" Uncle George asked.

Wilson shrugged. "Search me," he said. "I never saw anything special. The boy, Jerry, has some pretty wild friends, but they don't begin to circulate much till after I've gone for the day."

"About draining the pool yesterday," Uncle George said.

"Late afternoon," Wilson said. "There's a big maple tree near the pool. In the wind, day before yesterday, most of the leaves that were left dropped off the tree and a lot of them blew into the pool. Mr. Hopkins told me to drain it and get the leaves out. I did. It was nearly dark when I got through. I figured I wouldn't refill the pool till morning in case more leaves blew in. There wasn't any wind, so when I got there this morning I went to the pump house, turned on the water, waited to make sure the pump was working, and then went up to the pool. There she was, floating in about a foot of water."

"Blood?" Uncle George asked.

"If there was I didn't notice any. I was too busy shutting off the water, going to the house for help, getting her out of the pool."

ELORA PUBLIC LIBRARY
Elora, Mississippi

"How did the family react when they got the news?"

"Way you'd expect, I guess," Wilson said. "Mrs. Hopkins was hysterical. He, the boss, was rock hard. He said something like 'The stupid bitch didn't even look to see if the pool was empty.'"

"Anne didn't know you'd drained the pool?"

"She wasn't around. Like most of the town, she was up your road all afternoon, looking at that grave."

"Worked for the paper. She should have been there," Red said.

"Her clothes were in the bathhouse there?" Uncle George asked.

"I don't know for sure. I didn't have any reason to look there. I suppose they were. She wouldn't have been running around the grounds naked, even at that hour of the morning. House full of people."

"Late-night skinny-dips a regular thing out there?" Red Egan asked.

"I wasn't ever out there to witness one—if there was one," Wilson said. "I'd kinda doubt it was a regular thing, you know? People swimmin' naked in a place like Lakeview gets talked about, if it's known."

The phone on Red Egan's desk rang, and he answered. "Sheriff's office, Sheriff Egan speaking—for God's sake, Mark Kreevich! Sure I remember. About twenty-five years ago, wasn't it? You spent a couple of weeks here one summer with George Crowder when you were both in law school—matter of fact, he's sitting right here! Yeah, sure! Be great to see you." Egan handed the phone to Uncle George.

"Decided not to wait for your call, George," the homicide lieutenant said. "Duck soup down here. Telephone company gave me an address to go with that number. House in Greenwich Village—one-room apartments

40

occupied by mostly young people. Your Paul Comargo lives there, but nobody's seen him around for about a week. But you've got me hooked, George."

"Oh?"

"Still got some leaves to look at up there?"

"If you hurry."

"Like about three hours," Kreevich said. "Young fellow here who's a close friend of Comargo's. He's willing to ride up with me and take a look at what you've got in the morgue. If it turns out to be Paul Comargo, my young friend may have something to tell us both."

"I had a feeling you might strike gold," Uncle George said. "I'll be at the hospital when you get here."

Lieutenant Mark Kreevich was a dark, intense, wiry man with a smile that was rarely much warmer than a knife's edge. His main complaint in life was that, as a policeman, he found his main job was to solve crimes after they'd happened instead of preventing them. George Crowder had enormous respect for his old friend as a crime expert, and he chose not to let himself think that Kreevich's interest in the case was there only because an old friend was involved. Kreevich, hearing of this bizarre crime in the village of Lakeview, would recognize its "copycat" aspects—the old case in Texas—and would be asking himself when he might find a plastic tube protruding from a flower bed in Central Park attached to the coffin of a dead or dying man. Kreevich would want to know in advance everything there was to learn about this kind of pattern before it appeared in his own territory.

Kreevich had said "three hours" and Uncle George, knowing him, was at the hospital fifteen minutes sooner than that—just in time to see Kreevich and a young man with a thick black beard coming across the parking lot.

41

Some people promise to be somewhere at a certain time and are always late; Uncle George knew that Kreevich would give himself ample time and arrive a little early.

"You were right about the leaves," Kreevich said, as he shook hands with Uncle George on the front steps of the hospital. "Past their prime."

"So you will not be distracted," Uncle George said.

Kreevich introduced his companion. "This is Greg Lewis, George. Has the next apartment to Paul Comargo in the city. They're fairly close friends."

"Thanks for coming, Mr. Lewis," Uncle George said.

"When the lieutenant told me what you suspect, I had to come," Lewis said. His handshake was firm, his blue eyes bright and steady. It occurred to Uncle George that the bearded young men of today, hair worn long, all looked as if they were attempting some kind of disguise.

"Let's have a look at what you've got, George," Kreevich said. "We can talk afterwards. If it isn't Comargo there'll be nothing to talk about."

For the second time in a little more than twelve hours Uncle George took the elevator ride to the basement and went into the room where the sheet-covered body lay on a table. Young Greg Lewis walked over to the table and the attendant, a different one from the night before, pulled back the sheet. Lewis turned away in seconds, his face working.

"It's Paul," he said.

"No question?" Kreevich said.

"Hell, man, I've spent time with that guy almost every day of my life for more than a year. It's Paul Comargo, God help him."

They talked at first in Kreevich's car in the parking lot. Both Uncle George and the lieutenant wanted to hear what there was to know before they took Lewis to the State Police Barracks to make an official identification.

"I work for a business-machine company," Lewis told them. "Inter-office communicating systems, tabulators, electric typewriters, computers—the works. About fifteen months ago they hired a young guy named Paul Comargo. He was put under my wing to teach him the ropes. He knew computers inside out, highly qualified. And a nice guy!" Anger crept into Lewis's voice. "About a week after he was hired he was pink-slipped—fired. Someone higher up had fingered him. No reason. He was through, done, out!"

"Comargo knew why?" Uncle George asked.

"He didn't say then. I'd only known him for about a week. He was pretty bitter, and he said something like, 'I was warned, but I didn't believe it.' Maybe a month later I ran into Paul in a bar in the Village. He'd had quite a few. He told me it had happened to him again, that very day. Fired from his job without reason or explanation. He pointed to a dollar bill and some change on the bar. 'That's it,' he told me. 'You know some dark alley where I can bed down for the night?' I told him he could sleep on the couch in my apartment. He accepted, and that was the beginning of our being close for the next fourteen, fifteen months."

"And then he told you why?" Uncle George persisted.

Lewis nodded. "Girl he met in college," he said. "Her name was Anne, he told me. He was gone—hook, line, and sinker—on this girl. She had invited him to her country home for the weekend to meet her folks. It was that serious. She and her old man didn't hit it off. Paul didn't tell me the old man's name then, but it was Lucius Hopkins. This Hopkins told Paul to stay away from his daughter or else. Paul and the girl continued to meet and communicate, and boom, he was expelled from college! Came the job with my company, and he was dumped. Now he'd had a second time. I suggested no girl was worth that kind of harassment. He just said, 'I love her.' That was all. He got himself a job in the neighborhood loading and unloading trucks for a supermarket. Used another name. It didn't help. He was fired again. Hopkins must have had someone trailing him, knowing every move he made."

"All this time he was living with you?" Kreevich asked.

"He insisted on moving out. If I was helping him Hopkins might take a swipe at me. He was more than living with me, you understand. He was using my phone to keep in touch with his girl. She had a friend up here he could call, and she could call my phone to get him or leave a message for him with me."

"You talked to her?" Kreevich asked.

"Just to say hello, take a message," Lewis said. "God, what a way for her to go, and right after him!"

"She had to recognize him back there in the morgue?" Uncle George asked. "He isn't that badly disfigured?"

"Of course she knew him," Lewis said. "He looks like he'd been awful sick, but of course she knew it was him."

"She said not."

"She had her reasons, I suppose. The kind of job her old man had been doing on them—" Lewis shrugged.

"He moved out on you?" Kreevich asked.

"He finally got a job he wouldn't have taken under any other conditions, I think." Lewis frowned. "Flying a helicopter for some guys in the drug racket. They kept him under cover, I guess, because Hopkins didn't reach out for him there. The job provided him with some dough, and he rented a room in the same building with me. Be near my phone for messages. It's been that way for the last four or five months. No more trouble. Last Monday he told me he was coming up in this area to meet with his Anne. 'Be back the next day,' he told me. That's the last I ever saw of him."

"Can you name someone he was working for—this drug operation?" Kreevich asked.

Lewis gave the lieutenant a sour smile. "I can't, but if I

could I wouldn't. I'd kind of like to go on living, Lieutenant."

"Well, we'd better go see Captain Purdy and have Mr. Lewis identify his dead man for him," Red Egan said.

Uncle George got out of the car to head for his Jeep. "Speak to you two alone for a moment, Red?" he asked.

The sheriff and Lieutenant Kreevich joined him a few yards away from the car where Greg Lewis waited.

"You two willing to go for a lie which no one can catch you out in?" Uncle George asked.

"For a good cause," Kreevich said.

Uncle George looked steadily at his two friends. "Last night, after Anne Hopkins viewed the body in there—*and identified him for us*—she asked me to act for her as her lawyer."

"But she—" Red Egan began.

"She asked me to act for her and she told me much of what we've now heard from Lewis."

"Where does that get you, George?" Kreevich asked.

"My client is dead," Uncle George said, "but that doesn't relieve me of my commitment to her. That will justify my having it out with Lucius Hopkins."

Red Egan looked uncertain. "I don't know, George. People at the hospital know I was with you when we came here with Anne last night."

"But nobody but you knows that she didn't ask me for help before she left us to go home," Uncle George said. "Back me up and we've got a ball game going."

"I'd do it if I were you, Red," Mark Kreevich said. "Incidentally, I'm in on the case now."

"Not your jurisdiction," Red Egan said.

"Comargo was involved with the drug traffic in my area," Kreevich said. "That lets me in, friends."

Red Egan gave Uncle George a slow smile. "Go!" he said.

# 3

The old Crane place which Lucius Hopkins had bought some five years ago was situated just below the crest of a hill overlooking the town of Lakeview. The Crane family had built the graceful old Colonial house some sixty years ago and Cranes had always lived there until Silas Crane and his wife had died within a few months of each other. Lawyers had to sell it to settle the estate, and it went on the market, with a hundred acres of land surrounding it, for a staggering price. Lucius Hopkins, who as far as anyone locally knew had never been in the town of Lakeview before, was brought to see the house by an out-of-town real estate broker. He decided instantly that it was what he wanted and closed the deal. By the time he'd built a swimming pool, improved the roads through the property, repainted the house both inside and out, and, according to some local workmen, moved in a fortune in antique furniture and paintings and silver, the new Hopkins place involved an investment that ran well into seven figures.

Quite a few wealthy families had settled in Lakeview over the years, mostly people of retirement age, but the Hopkinses had outdistanced all of them in what they had spent for a place to live. Bits and pieces of information about them had been accumulated by curious locals. To begin with, Lucius Hopkins and his wife were not of retirement age. Hopkins, looking a little like a prematurely gray Clark Gable, was not more than fifty, a man of enormous vitality. He was clearly still actively involved in the corporate ventures that had made him so rich. He was constantly back and forth in a private plane which he kept in a hangar on the hilltop and which he flew himself. A mechanic who

46

had been brought in from out of town to keep the plane in working order also kept a half a dozen cars in shape, and, like the other out-of-town employees on the estate, didn't mix with local people or gossip or talk about his employers.

The family consisted of Hopkins and his wife, Delia, and two children, Jerry, the son in his early twenties, and until today Anne, the daughter a couple of years younger than her brother. As far as Uncle George knew no one had been aware that Anne was not Hopkins's daughter. Possibly Marilyn Stroud, who had been so close to Anne, had been told, but she had kept that information to herself as she'd obviously been requested to do. It was all going to come out now, Uncle George knew, and wondered what more with it?

Efforts to make friends and be neighborly by other residents of Lakeview had been resisted. Not anyone in town had managed to get close to any of the Hopkinses except, it now seemed, Marilyn Stroud, and that friendship between the young girl and the older woman had evidently been carried on in secret. Hopkins, when he first came to town, had been asked to serve on the hospital board. He'd refused, but had made a rather generous contribution to the institution. Any approach toward friendship, however, had been met with bruskness and downright discourtesy. The local ladies had tried to interest Delia Hopkins in the garden club and the church but were turned away, not impolitely, on the grounds that ill health made Mrs. Hopkins something of a shut-in. What her health problems were no one knew. If she saw a doctor he was from out of town. Doc Walters, the local man, had never been called to see her.

The two children reached early maturity in Lakeview, but were away at school and college most of each year. Jerry, a younger edition of his father, raced around town in the summer months, ignoring the speed limits in his sports car, accused of rowdiness in some of the outlying bars

47

where he went with his out-of-town friends who visited Hilltop, the name given the old Crane place by its new owners. Jerry was arrested several times for speeding, for brawling, and once for vandalism at a synagogue in a neighboring town. He paid the fines, and avoided a jail sentence for the vandalism with the aid of an out-of-town lawyer who charged the town with prejudice against "outsiders."

Anne, people had said, was "the only human being in the lot." She was quiet, friendly, spoke to people on the street, was particularly good with children, and had obviously made an important friend in Marilyn Stroud. "Seems like she's trying to make up for the way the other ones are," someone had said. Well, she had made it and she was tragically gone.

Uncle George drove his Jeep up to the big iron gates that blocked the entrance to Hilltop. They were closed and locked. On the right gate post was an electric bell with a little brass sign on it. Uncle George rang the bell and waited. Presently, down from the house, came an electric golf cart driven by a man Uncle George recognized as the mechanic who took care of the Hopkins cars and the plane. He was a dark-haired, narrow-eyed young man.

"You want something?" he asked.

"I want to talk to Mrs. Hopkins," Uncle George said.

"You local?"

"Yes."

"Then you know what's happened here?"

"To Anne Hopkins? Yes."

"Then you know Mrs. Hopkins doesn't want to talk to anyone," the man said. "You better go peddle your papers, buster."

"You know what happened here yesterday, across the valley from here?" Uncle George asked. "Man buried alive?"

"Hell, yes. It's been on radio and TV till it comes out of your ears," the man said.

"I'm the man who found him," Uncle George said. "Last night, not long before she died, Anne Hopkins identified the man for me and the sheriff. He'd been a guest here one weekend, some time back. With Anne gone it's necessary for Mr. and Mrs. Hopkins to get involved."

"Give them time to get over what's happened to them," the man said.

"I suggest you let me in," Uncle George said, "or I'll come back with the State Police and we'll take your gate right off its hinges if we have to—buster!"

Just then a car came speeding down from the area of the house. It was a fire-engine red Porsche convertible. Uncle George recognized the young man at the wheel as Jerry Hopkins, the son of the household. His dark hair was worn longish, and he'd obviously spent most of the summer out in the sun. He was tanned a mahogany brown.

"What's wrong here, Ed?" he asked the mechanic.

"This old coot seems to think he's got to see Mrs. Hopkins," the mechanic said.

"You're George Crowder, aren't you?" young Hopkins asked. "Been seeing you on television since yesterday. You must know what's happened to us here and that my father and mother are entitled to a little privacy."

"Very shortly privacy isn't going to be possible," Uncle George said. "Police and an army of reporters and photographers are going to be bearing down on you."

"Why?"

"Last night—or rather, early this morning—your sister asked to see the body of the man we found buried on my property across the valley."

"Good God, why? I suppose she was trying to be a big-shot reporter for the local paper."

49

"She thought he might be someone she knew and cared for," Uncle George said, his voice a kind of deadly quiet. "It turned out that's who he was, a young man named Paul Comargo."

"Anne told you that?"

"And another witness, a friend of Comargo's, has just verified it for the sheriff. They've gone to report to the State Police, and they'll all be bearing down on you presently."

The young man's face had gone grim. "And why have you come on ahead of them, Mr. Crowder?"

"This morning, just before she left the hospital to come home here, your sister asked me to be her attorney, her lawyer, to represent her interests in the case."

"They said on TV you are a lawyer, retired. Why did Anne need your help?"

"Because the man she loved had been murdered. And because for a long time your father has been taking potshots at him, your sister felt she needed outside help."

"She thought Dad had something to do with that monstrous business on your property?"

"And the police will, at least, be interested when they hear her story."

"From you?"

"Since she can no longer tell them herself," Uncle George said.

"You think my father arranged to have this Comargo creep buried alive?" Jerry Hopkins sounded as though he was fighting laughter.

"I think she didn't go straight to the police because she wanted to talk to her mother first. She knew how deeply fond of her stepfather her mother is."

"She told you Dad isn't her real father?"

Uncle George nodded. "I think she wanted to forewarn her mother of what she intended to tell the police."

"What hogwash!" Jerry Hopkins exploded. "Well, un-happily, Anne's dead. So you don't have a client any longer."

"My obligation to help her is still very much alive, Jerry. I want to prepare her mother just as she meant to prepare her. If you want the roof to cave in on her without any warning of what's coming, that's up to you."

"And you plan to keep your nose stuck in our business, even though Anne isn't here to need you?"

"Something like that," Uncle George said.

The young man turned to the mechanic. "Let him in. I think my father should have this out with you, Mr. Crowder. Follow me."

Some years ago Uncle George had been inside the big house on the hill for some kind of open house given by the Cranes. He felt a little shocked as he waited in the wide entrance hall for Jerry Hopkins to find his father. On that first visit he had been impressed with the mute-white woodwork, the antique wall papers, the almost historic perfection of the old house. It had been transformed by the Hopkinses. The wallpaper was gone, replaced by a variety of garishly painted panels. The white of the woodwork was new, new, new. None of the traditional New England patina was left. It looked, Uncle George thought, like a modern nightclub or casino.

Jerry Hopkins had gone to a door at the far end of the big entrance hall and he returned now with his father. Uncle George remembered his earlier impression of a prema-turely gray Clark Gable, but a Gable in a cold, angry mood at this moment.

"I know who you are, Crowder," he said. He turned to his son. "Get Forsythe on the phone for me, Jerry. I'll be in the study."

Jerry gave Uncle George a sort of cavalier wave of good-bye, as if to say, "Now you'll find out what the score is."

51

"This way," Lucius Hopkins said. "I don't want the whole damned household to hear whatever it is you have to say, Crowder."

The study at the end of the hall was lined with bookcases and filing cabinets. This was a work place without any show-off qualities for the casual visitor. Just outside the picture window at the far end was the swimming pool, surrounded by old maple trees, where Anne Hopkins was said to have died. It was still empty, as it must have been when she made her fatal dive. If, Uncle George told himself, she *did* make a fatal dive.

"I'll not ask you to sit, Crowder," Hopkins said, "because I don't have the time—or the stomach—to discuss the kind of nonsense Jerry says you're here about. My daughter is dead. Whatever nonsensical arrangement she may have made with you is obviously no longer in effect. I'm talking to you only to tell you that if you try to spread the malicious garbage you mentioned to Jerry I promise you I will make you wish you had never been born."

"I've wished that once before in my life," Uncle George said.

"Yes, I understand you are a discredited lawyer."

"Discredited by myself, but not the bar association, Mr. Hopkins. I'm still licensed to practice law in this state, and I still have an obligation to my client, in spite of what has happened to her."

"Obligation to do what?"

"Investigate the matter of her young man and see that justice is done on his behalf—and now, perhaps, hers.

"I was with Anne at shortly after two this morning. I watched her leave the hospital and head for home—for here. I know that she was in shock. She'd just seen the young man with whom she was in love lying on a slab in the hospital morgue. She was just about as likely to go for a relaxing swim in freezing weather as I am to take off from this room and fly to the moon."

52

A nerve twitched high up on Hopkins's cheek. "Are you suggesting that—"

"I'm suggesting that we're confronted by too damned many unanswered questions, Hopkins," Uncle George said. "I chose to let you answer some of them in private. I think Anne would have wanted her mother protected from as much scandalous gossip as she could be. That might not be possible if I go to the State Police with my questions. It's up to you, for the time being, whether you want it private or public."

Hopkins was clearly trying to make an assessment of the tall gray man who was facing him. Perhaps he was aware that George Crowder was not some kind of local "character," that there was steel behind the level eyes, the quiet voice. Making the correct judgments about people had probably helped to make Hopkins a very rich man.

"Sit down, Mr. Crowder," he said. "Ask what you want to ask."

The chromium-plated armchair that belonged in a modern apartment and not an old Colonial mansion somehow made Uncle George hesitate. But he sat, and was surprised to find the angularly designed chair quite comfortable.

"You knew that the man who was found buried on my property yesterday was Paul Comargo?" he asked.

"I knew it ten minutes ago when Jerry told me you'd told him," Hopkins said. "I suppose it's been on radio and television, but as you can imagine we haven't been sitting around, listening to the news, in this household, Crowder. We've had our own tragedy. Mrs. Hopkins is, quite naturally, devastated by what's happened. Our daughter—"

"Mrs. Hopkins's daughter," Uncle George interrupted.

Hopkins looked genuinely surprised. "Anne told you that?"

"Last night—or this morning."

"It was kept a secret to protect Anne, give her the prestige of the Hopkins name. If Anne chose to tell you that she

53

was not my daughter there's no reason to keep it a secret. There was nothing shameful, or illegal, or improper about it. She was less than a year old when I married her mother and adopted her. Nothing in that to interest her lawyer—if it turns out you really are her lawyer, Crowder."

"You had a falling out with Anne over Paul Comargo about a year and a half ago?"

"I certainly did," Hopkins said, his eyes glittering in the light from the window overlooking the pool where Anne had died only hours ago. "He was a no-good street kid with nothing on earth to offer Anne, and with the impertinence to tell me I had no right to interfere in his friendship—he called it 'friendship'—with Anne. You spend your life trying to protect your kids from cheap, shoddy entanglements, and then, overnight, your daughter is in the hay with a louse who sees the Hopkins money at the end of his romance."

"They told you they were lovers?"

"Like hell they told me! I suspected. I walked into Anne's room in the middle of the night that weekend Comargo came here, found him in bed with her, slavering over her naked body! I ordered him out of the house, warned him that if he ever tried to see Anne again he'd discover just what kind of heat I could bring to bear on him."

"And when he did see Anne you got him expelled from college, had him fired from two or three jobs, and when you heard he was here in town last Monday to see Anne you decided to show him just how hot that heat you were talking about could be."

Hopkins's hands, holding the back of the chair behind which he was standing, tightened so hard that his knuckles looked like a row of white marbles. "Are you suggesting that I—" It was almost a whisper.

"Bound hand and foot," Uncle George said quietly. "Placed in a box, nails driven in from the outside so that if

54

he moved, his flesh would be torn, a plastic tube placed in his mouth, the top nailed on the box, and buried alive for five days—just a matter of minutes too long for him to survive. That really is what I'd call 'heat,' Mr. Hopkins."

Hopkins's legs seemed to buckle under him and he moved around to sink into his chair. "And you think—"

"I came here to ask," Uncle George said.

"My God!" Hopkins said.

"Anne obviously believed it was possible," Uncle George said, "which is why she asked the sheriff to let her see the body. When she saw that it was her man who'd been so brutally murdered she asked me for help." It wasn't quite the true sequence but it had the ring of truth to it.

"And you didn't urge her to go to the police then?" Hopkins asked.

"I think she wanted to talk to her mother, first."

That nerve twitched again in Hopkins's cheek. "You know that we didn't know where she was, that she *had* come home, until Jake Wilson woke us with the dreadful news that she was in the pool, dead?"

"I know that's what Wilson says."

"For God's sake, man, it's true! Mrs. Hopkins can tell you that. We—we sleep together. We went to bed about eleven thirty. We'd stayed up later than usual, thinking Anne, working for the local paper, might get home with more about what we'd been hearing on television. She didn't come. Delia and I slept till we were wakened by the maid, who'd been alerted by Wilson."

"So she can't tell anyone her suspicions now," Uncle George said. "Fortunately she let us know what they were before she died."

"Fortunately?" Hopkins laughed. He was not a man to be floored by one punch. "Let me lay it on the line for you, Crowder, and then I'm through talking to you or anyone else without my lawyer being present."

"That's probably sensible," Uncle George said.

55

"You suggest that I knew Anne was seeing that Comargo after I'd run him out of the house here. I assumed she was doing what I'd ordered her to do—cut all ties with that creep. I didn't know they were seeing each other, certainly had no idea they were planning to meet here last Monday or Tuesday. You suggest I had Comargo expelled from college. I did not. You should be able to check with the authorities at Skidmore to verify that. You suggest I had him fired from several jobs. I have no idea where he may have been working so I can't suggest where you check on that. Friends of his in the city might help you there. The notion that I could have been involved in or ordered that grotesque torture and murder would be funny if it wasn't almost criminally irresponsible." The phone rang on the desk and Hopkins lifted the receiver. "Yes? Oh, hello, Logan. Hold on for a moment, will you?" Hopkins covered the mouthpiece with his hand. "This is Logan Forsythe, my lawyer. I'd like to talk with him in private. So, if you will excuse me, Crowder—"

Uncle George walked out of the study and into the garish entrance hall. Jerry Hopkins was there, cigarette between his lips, obviously waiting for him.

"Dad set you straight, Crowder?" he asked.

"He told me his story," Uncle George said.

"So I'll take pleasure in showing you off the grounds," Jerry said, with the white, mirthless smile that was a copy of his father's.

"I'd like to see the bathhouse where Anne changed out of her clothes before she made her fatal dive." Uncle George said.

"I don't think I'm authorized to give you the guided tour, Crowder," Jerry said.

"The State Police should be here in a few minutes with a warrant to search the whole place," Uncle George said.

"Search for what?"

Uncle George's voice was harsh. "For bits of lumber

56

from which a coffin was made; for nails that match the ones that were driven into that coffin to torture a man; for bits of plastic tubing that was used to keep a man alive longer that he could bear being buried alive; and—I think—to examine the circumstances of Anne's death."

"You're off your rocker, Crowder! Your marbles are scrambled! Anne, crazy kid, didn't bother to look to see if there was any water in the pool. What's the bathhouse got to do with it?"

"Her clothes," Uncle George said. "I'd like to see them."

"She wasn't wearing clothes. She'd stripped."

"I'd still like to see her clothes."

"What you're going to see is the front gate," Jerry said. "Let's not have any more of this crap, Crowder."

"Jerry!"

It was a woman's voice. Both men turned and Uncle George recognized Delia Hopkins. She was, he guessed, about forty. Her fair hair looked to be the result of an expert rinse. She was wearing a dark wool dress, and her normally pretty face looked crumpled by grief.

"I apologize for Jerry's rudeness, Mr. Crowder," she said. "What is it that you wanted from him?"

"Since you know who I am, Mrs. Hopkins, you must also know what was found on my property yesterday."

"I know you from seeing you in town, asking about you," Delia Hopkins said. "I also know what happened to you from watching television last night. We both seem to have been subjected to unbelievable horror."

"Yours is much more personal than mine, Mrs. Hopkins. Have you heard this morning that the dead man on my property is—was—Paul Comargo?"

"Oh, my God! Anne's friend?"

"I'm afraid so, Mrs. Hopkins. She went to the hospital early this morning and identified him. It was then that she asked me to act for her—as her lawyer."

"Why on earth would she want a lawyer, Mr. Crowder?"

57

Something like bitterness crept into her voice. "God knows we have lawyers enough in and out of the Hopkins world."

"But not lawyers who would concern themselves with Paul Comargo's interests. According to Anne her step-father had made Comargo's life about unlivable for the last year and a half. She evidently thought Comargo would be better served by someone who wouldn't be taking orders from that stepfather. Now that both Comargo and Anne are gone I don't feel my responsibility to them is gone."

"What is it you can do for Anne?" the woman asked.

"Make absolutely certain that her death was an accident," Uncle George said.

"My God, Mr. Crowder!"

"Some sadistic, psychotic person in this area tortured and murdered Paul Comargo. Anne was out to get justice for her friend. Someone could have decided to stop her before she really got started. I was with her, probably less than an hour before she died. I find it hard to believe that taking a swim on a cold, fall night was a part of her program."

"Anne was always erratic," Jerry Hopkins said.

"Please be still, Jerry," Delia Hopkins said. Her face had taken on a kind of frozen look. "What were you asking Jerry when I came in, Mr. Crowder?"

"I want to see the bathhouse where Anne is supposed to have undressed and taken her dive into the pool."

"Why?"

"I wanted to see her clothes, Mrs. Hopkins."

"Why?"

"Because if Anne was harmed on her way home this morning, if her body in the pool was just a camouflage for an injury inflicted some other way, then her clothes might tell us something."

"How could they tell us anything?"

"Bloodstains, torn material—I don't really know, but I'd like to look."

58

Delia Hopkins took a deep breath. "Follow me, Mr. Crowder."

"Dad isn't going to like this," Jerry Hopkins warned. "Crowder doesn't have the legal right to investigate anything here."

Delia Hopkins gave her stepson a cold look. "He does now, Jerry. I give it to him. Come with me, Mr. Crowder."

French doors at the far end of the entrance hall opened onto a flagstone path. A short walk through a vine-covered arbor led to the bathhouse. Like everything else at Hilltop the bathhouse was elaborately modern on the inside. There were four dressing cubicles, each with a shower attached, and shelves loaded with fresh towels. There were two massage tables, a sunlamp in place over each one. There was a cabinet containing bathing caps for ladies with hairdos to preserve—or men with hairdos to preserve, for that matter.

In the second cubicle were clothes—tan shirtwaist, a corduroy skirt, underpanties, navy-blue socks and a pair of moccasin-type shoes. A sheepskin-lined car coat was on a separate hook.

"Anne's things," Mrs. Hopkins said, in a low voice.

Uncle George didn't move from where he stood just outside the cubicle. "I can't be sure about the shoes, the socks, and the underpants," he said. "But the shirtwaist, the skirt, and the car coat are not what she was wearing when she left me at the hospital. She was wearing a pink man's shirt, navy-blue slacks, and a blue quilted jacket."

"So she came home, changed, decided to go for a swim, and came down here," Jerry said. He had followed them from the main house.

"She changed to go somewhere?" Uncle George asked. "At two-thirty in the morning?"

"Maybe to the police," Delia Hopkins said.

"Then we'll find the things she was wearing when she left me up in her room," Uncle George said.

"I remember she went out wearing those blue slacks and the pink shirt," Delia Hopkins said. "You're right. They'll be up in her room."

"Is—is she there?" Uncle George asked.

"No, no. She's still at the undertakers. They—they have considerable work to do to make her look presentable. Her head—her face."

"Can we look at the clothes? The clothes in her room?"

"Of course."

"I warn you, Crowder, my father's going to have your hide for this," Jerry Hopkins said.

"It will have to be my hide, Jerry, not Mr. Crowder's," Delia Hopkins said.

They went back to the house, across the entrance hall, up a wide, winding staircase to the second floor. Anne's room was at the end of the hall. Uncle George was aware of the faint scent of a delicate perfume as he followed Delia Hopkins in. A woman's room, but scrupulously neat. It occurred to him that in the course of this tragic day for the Hopkinses, Anne's room had been given special care. There was nothing wrong or unusual, in the circumstances, about that. Captain Purdy of the State Police might not like it, however, if he began to think along the same lines as Uncle George.

"A very neat young lady," Uncle George said. "Or has this room been given special treatment?"

Delia Hopkins faced the tall gray man. They were alone, Jerry having gone off somewhere, probably to tell his father what was happening. "You keep implying that Anne didn't—wasn't—"

"A prosecuting attorney's mind, Mrs. Hopkins. I once held that job in this county."

"I know. I'd heard."

"Then you know," Uncle George said, "that I'm not always right. The clothes Anne was wearing when I saw her would have been put away somewhere?"

"Hilda Clarkson, the housemaid, was ordered to put Anne's room in order. We—we plan to bring Anne home, to her own room, for a day or two before—before funeral arrangements are made. Hilda very likely put Anne's discarded clothes in the laundry."

"You send laundry out?"

"No, we do everything here. There's a laundry in the basement."

"Could you ask Hilda to find those clothes for us—if that's where they are?"

"Of course."

"The blue quilted jacket she was wearing; would that go to the laundry, too?"

Delia Hopkins turned around and went to a big walk-in closet at the end of the room. Dresses, coats, sweaters were hung there. Delia looked, moving clothes on their hangers.

"It doesn't seem to be here," she said. "Hilda may have taken it to the downstairs coat closet where all of us hang our outdoor things."

"Ask the maid about it, please."

Left alone, Uncle George realized that old, almost forgotten habits had overtaken him. He was, as he'd suggested to Delia Hopkins, thinking like a cop. A persistent hunch that refused to be put aside told him that Anne Hopkins's naked plunge into the pool had not been a tragic accident. Hunch told him that it was murder, committed somewhere else, her body stripped of clothing that would have told a story of violence and thrown into the pool so that a fatal head injury would appear to have been accidental. Proof? Not a shred of it yet—just hunch.

"Damned old fool," Uncle George told himself, even though his hunch told him that he was not.

He walked over to the closet and stood looking at a young woman's wardrobe. The neatness bothered him; so very neat for an active, busy girl; everything washed, cleaned, waiting to be worn. He noticed a robe and a night-gown hanging together on a hook. He took the silk night-gown in his fingers and sniffed at it. The scent of perfume was there. Not washed since it was last worn, he thought. He took it down, rolled it into a small, tight ball, and stuffed it into the pocket of his car coat. As he turned away Delia Hopkins came back into the room with a blond girl in a pale blue maid's uniform and apron.

"This is Hilda Clarkson, Mr. Crowder."

"Do you mind answering a couple of simple questions, Hilda?" Uncle George asked.

"No, sir."

"I understand you were told to put this room in order after the accident to Miss Hopkins was discovered."

"Taking care of Miss Anne's room is one of my regular routines," the girl said. "Making her bed, changing the sheets and pillow cases twice a week, picking up after her, vacuuming, cleaning the bathroom."

"You say 'picking up after her,' Hilda. Anne leave things pretty messy?"

"Oh, no. I—I wish it was easy for me to be as orderly as she was. But she would leave out clothes that were to go to the laundry, or to the cleaners. Maybe she'd leave clothes hanging over a chair instead of in the closet."

"The clothes she was wearing when she came home last night—blue slacks, a pink man's shirt, a quilted blue jacket; you found them here this morning?"

The girl glanced at Delia Hopkins. "I told Mrs. Hopkins they weren't anywhere here, nor in the laundry hamper in the bathroom. She could have left the jacket in the hall closet downstairs."

"But it isn't there," Delia Hopkins said.

"Can either of you suggest what might have happened to them that you haven't thought of? Could they have gone to the cleaners?"

"This is Tuesday," Hilda said. "The cleaners come Wednesdays and Saturdays. When Mrs. Hopkins first asked me I supposed Miss Anne's clothes were down in the pool house—the bathhouse."

"Not the same clothes," Delia Hopkins said in a voice that had taken on a flat, dead sound.

"It would seem that Anne came home, changed out of those blue things and the pink shirt, into a corduroy skirt, a tan shirtwaist, and a sheepskin-lined car coat. Went out again, decided to go for a swim, undressed again, and—and dove into an empty pool."

"It doesn't make sense," Delia Hopkins said.

"I'm afraid I don't think it does, either," Uncle George said. "Hilda, will you search for those missing clothes? They could, I suppose, have been taken somewhere by someone, misplaced. Things must have been pretty hysterical around here when Anne's body was discovered by Jake Wilson. Someone could, I suppose, have glanced in here, seen clothes lying on the floor, on a chair, on the bed, picked them up and dumped them in another laundry hamper, in another room."

"I don't know where to look, sir," the maid said, "but I'll do the best I can." She took off, leaving Uncle George alone with Delia Hopkins.

"When I got here this afternoon, Mrs. Hopkins, the front gate was locked. Is that standard practice at Hilltop?"

"Not in the daytime," Delia said. "But today— sightseers, the press—Lucius didn't want people just coming and going at will."

"At night—normally?"

"As you know, Mr. Crowder, Lucius has a fabulous collection of paintings and sculpture, tempting for any kind of thief. Unless we have a party, or house guests who may want to come and go, the gates are locked at ten o'clock. There is a night watchman, a man named Joe Bradshaw.

He patrols the inside grounds two or three times a night, and if anyone comes to the gates and rings the bell he answers it."

"Anne left me in town a little after two in the morning," Uncle George said. "When she got home she had to summon Bradshaw to get through the gates?"

Delia shook her head slowly. "The family members—Lucius, Jerry, Anne, me, some of the servants—all have keys to the gate. Ann wouldn't have had to call Bradshaw."

"Her car? As I remember she was driving a Mustang convertible."

"It's in the garage. I heard Jake Wilson report that to Lucius."

"Then Bradshaw, if he was up and around, would have known that some family member had come home, unlocked the gates, and driven to the garage?"

"Yes."

"He would have known who was out and who might be coming back?"

"Yes, I think he would. There wasn't any reason to ask him, I guess. I mean, Anne was there—in the pool—Jerry was home, Lucius and I had never been out at all."

"Can we talk to Bradshaw?"

"Come with me," Delia said.

She led the way, this time down a back stairway that led to the kitchen area. A woman cook and another housemaid watched them walk through the kitchen and out into what was, in season, a neat kitchen garden. About fifty yards from the main house was a small cottage. Two men were sitting on a bench outside the cottage. One of them was Jake Wilson, whom Uncle George knew. The other was a slim, blond young man. A boxer dog sat at his knee, a chain choke-collar in place. As Delia and Uncle George approached, the dog stood up, a deep, warning growl coming from his throat.

"It's all right, Charlie," the blond man said. "Just sit and and stay."

Uncle George and Delia reached the two men, who stood up in deference to Delia. Uncle George's right hand reached down toward the boxer's tan head. The dog growled but Uncle George didn't move his hand.

"You're apt to get your arm taken off if you try that kind of thing," the blond man said.

"I'll chance it," Uncle George said. He didn't move his hand.

"Mr. Crowder wants to ask you some questions, Bradshaw," Delia said.

"Mr. Hopkins told me I wasn't to talk to anyone about last night, Mrs. Hopkins," Bradshaw said.

The young man had gray-green eyes that seemed, Uncle George thought, to be on the constant lookout for trouble.

"I'd like you to tell Mr. Crowder what he wants to know," Delia said.

Bradshaw's nervous eyes turned to Uncle George. "So?" he said.

"You know when Anne came home last night?" Uncle George asked.

"I knew that Anne or Jerry came in about four o'clock," Bradshaw said.

"Four o'clock?"

Bradshaw nodded. "I knew they were both out. I make rounds just before midnight, or whenever house guests have all left if there is a party. I make a second round about three-thirty. I was out at the far end of the place when I saw headlights at the gates. I figured it was Jerry. He's often out that late. I saw the headlights come up the drive to the garage so I knew he'd let himself in. When I got back down here I looked in the garage and I saw that it was Anne's car, not Jerry's, that had come in."

"And when did Jerry come home?"

Bradshaw shrugged. "His car was there, too."

"When? At four o'clock?"

"I don't know for sure. When I saw Anne's car I didn't look for his. He could have come in before when I was lying down in the cottage. Charlie wouldn't bark at him." He looked down at his dog and showed surprise. The boxer was gently licking Uncle George's hand. He gave a sharp yank at the leash, jerking the dog's head away. "When Jake, here, sounded the alarm about Miss Anne being in the pool, I looked in the garage. Jerry's car was there, but I don't know for sure when he came home. You must know, Mrs. Hopkins. You'd hear him in the house, wouldn't you?"

"I heard him," Delia said, "but I didn't check on the time. It's always late."

"The question is," Uncle George said, "where was Anne between two, when she left me at the hospital, and four when Bradshaw saw her car come in? It's about a mile and a half from the hospital to here."

"Wherever she was is none of your business, Crowder!" Lucius Hopkins had come around the corner of the big house, unnoticed by the others. "I told you not to talk to anyone, Bradshaw. And you, Jake."

"Mrs. Hopkins told me—" Bradshaw began.

"You take your orders from me and no one else," Hopkins said. "And now, Crowder, we've had enough of your meddling for one day. And you, Delia, please go to the house and leave this matter to me."

Delia didn't move. "I want you to hear what Mr. Crowder is thinking, Lucius," she said.

"I don't give a damn what Crowder is thinking," Hopkins said. "And now, do I need help in getting you to leave my property, Crowder?"

"There are some questions that need answering, Lucius," Delia said. She was showing unexpected resistance to her husband's orders.

66

"Let them be asked by someone with the proper authority!" Hopkins said. He turned and called out, "Captain Purdy!"

The kitchen door opened and Captain Purdy of the State Police came across the lawn to where the others stood. He looked a little sheepish.

"I'm sorry, George," he said. "Mr. Hopkins says you are trespassing. He has a right to ask you to leave." The trooper captain's smile was tight. "You didn't want to be hampered by regulations, remember?"

"Mr. Crowder is Anne's lawyer, Captain," Delia Hopkins said.

"Was Anne's lawyer," Hopkins said, "if—if he ever *was* Anne's lawyer."

"Then, if he will, I am asking him to be my lawyer," Delia said.

"Oh, for God's sake, Delia!" Hopkins said.

"I'll be glad to act for you if you find you need a lawyer, Mrs. Hopkins," Uncle George said. "Meanwhile, perhaps if I leave, Captain Purdy will be able to get on with what he should be doing, which is solving two bizarre murders."

"Two murders?" Hopkins said, anger mounting.

"That, of course, is just my opinion, Mr. Hopkins. I know you're not interested in my opinion." Uncle George grinned at Captain Purdy. "I'll go quietly, officer—unless you want to hold my hand until I get outside the gates."

Captain Purdy did follow Uncle George to the front of the house where the Jeep was parked.

"What are you talking about—two murders, George?" he asked.

"Just one of my unreliable hunches, Jim. But you might try to find the answers to some questions. For instance, where are the clothes Anne Hopkins was wearing when she left Red and me at the hospital after viewing Comargo's body? Blue slacks, a pink shirt, a blue quilted jacket. They're not in her room, they're not in the bathhouse.

67

They're not in the laundry hamper or in the closets where they should be."

"She was naked when she was found in the pool by Wilson."

"So she had discarded the clothes she was wearing at the hospital and different clothes were hanging in the dressing cubicle in the bathhouse. If she changed, where are the clothes she changed out of?"

"You said 'questions,' plural."

"Anne left Red and me at the hospital a little after two o'clock. Bradshaw says she got home around four. A mile and a half she could have driven in five minutes. Where was she for almost two hours?"

Purdy was frowning. "Anything else?"

"Did Doc Walters do an autopsy on Anne, or did you all just assume she smashed in her skull diving into an empty pool? Other injuries? Could she, for example, have been drugged, poisoned? In short, Jim, was the whole thing carefully staged so that you wouldn't look for the truth?"

"Honestly, George, that is pretty far out, isn't it?"

"I'll leave you with one more," Uncle George said. "Bradshaw was patrolling the grounds at four o'clock when, from a distance, he saw car headlights at the gates, and then they came up the driveway to the garage. It had to be one of the family who had a key to the gates. When he got back to the garage he saw Anne's car and assumed she'd been the late arrival. But he didn't see Anne. Someone else—with a key—could have brought her car home. He added up two and two, and maybe it came up five."

"You're suggesting that—"

"That someone else brought Anne's car home. I might go further, and guess that she was in it, dead. That she was planted in the pool."

Captain Purdy shook his head. "George, you better go home and get some rest. The last twenty-four hours have been too much for you."

Uncle George got into his Jeep and started the engine.
"You go to your church, Jim, and I'll go to mine," he said.

There was one question Uncle George hadn't suggested
to Captain Purdy that needed answering. Most of the day
he had involved himself in what he chose to think of as a
"white lie." He had let the Hopkins household believe that
Anne had identified Paul Comargo in the hospital morgue.
Anne hadn't made an identification in words; in fact she
had denied knowing the dead man on the morgue table.
But as far as Uncle George and Red Egan were concerned
her instant reaction, when the attendant pulled back the
sheet from the corpse's face, had been all the identification
they needed. The dead man was her guy, the man she
loved.

That left the question Uncle George hadn't posed to
Captain Purdy. Why had she pretended not to know Comargo? Why had she refused the help that was there to be
given? What had she planned to do about it herself? She'd
had some plan in mind, something she thought could or
should be done before Comargo was certainly identified in
the morning by her stepfather, her mother, one of the
servants. What had she wanted to do in those early hours of
the morning before the truth came out? Confront someone
she suspected of a sadistic murder? Produce some evidence
she'd known about before the killer could take flight? Warn
someone she thought might be on a monster's hit-list?

The fall afternoon was fading fast when Uncle George
drove up the logging road to his cabin. He was surprised
not to see Timmy waiting for him on the front doorstep;
and realized almost at once that he had company—familiar
company—and that Timmy was inside the house. Joey
Trimble, his beloved nephew, had a key to the Yale lock on
the cabin door.

Boy and dog greeted him with enthusiasm. The boy
bursting with questions about the "crime," the dog de-

manding reassurance that came with a rubbing behind his ears and a momentary chance to swipe at his owner's cheek with an affectionate tongue.

"I almost forgot," Joey said. "Pop sent me with a message for you, Uncle George."

"What have I done wrong now?" Uncle George asked, his smile wry.

"Nothing like that. Mom's at the Garden Club meeting and it seems Miss Stroud called and said she needed to see you. Something urgent, Pop said to tell you."

There was no telephone at the cabin. Reaching Uncle George through Esther was Marilyn Stroud's best chance.

"But before you go, Uncle George, is there anything new? About the murder? Have the police come up with anything? More important, have you come up with anything?"

Uncle George rumpled the boy's hair. "A complex case, Watson, very complex," he said.

"But you have a theory, Holmes?" the boy asked.

"You've heard me talk about Mark Kreevich, my friend on the Homicide squad in New York?"

"Of course!"

"Mark has come up with a man who was able to identify the man in the box. It turns out he was Anne Hopkins's boyfriend, name of Paul Comargo."

"Oh, wow!" Dr. Watson said.

"That's had me wondering what really happened to Anne. I don't think it was an accident, Watson."

"Oh, wow, Holmes!"

"I think something happened to her between the time she left Red and me at the hospital at two o'clock in the morning and when they say she got home two hours later." From the pocket of his parka Uncle George took the crumpled silk nightgown he'd taken from Anne's clothes closet in her room at Hilltop. "This belonged to Anne. I planned to let Timmy have a smell of it, and then take him down to the hospital and walk both sides of the road—see if he can pick up anything. Anne may have stopped, been forced out of her car, who knows what. Timmy may be helpful."

"Oh, wow, Holmes. Can I go with you?"

"I'm afraid it's going to have to wait, Watson. Marilyn Stroud wouldn't have sent for me if she didn't have something important." Uncle George held the rolled-up nightgown down for Timmy to sniff. "I'll drive you back to town, Joey, if you want."

"I don't have to be home till six," Joey said. "I'll wait for you to hear what's up, if that's okay."

"Why not. But keep track of the time, boy. You know how your old man is. You're late and you won't eat." Uncle George tossed the nightgown onto the table by the couch. "You stay here with Joey, Tim." He turned back to his nephew. "There are some baked ham slices, bread, and milk in case you get hungry—or late," he said.

In late October the sun was gone by four-thirty in the afternoon. Lights were on in houses all along the main street of the village as Uncle George drove his Jeep to the little cottage, not far from the school, where Marilyn Stroud lived. There the windows were dark. Marilyn, he thought, had gone somewhere, but to be sure he went to the front door and knocked. He was just about to turn away when he heard a tense, frightened voice from inside the cottage.

"Who is it?"

"Marilyn? It's George Crowder."

"Just a minute, George."

He heard the lock being turned, the clank of an inside chain lock. The door opened and Marilyn asked him to "come in" in that same tense voice.

Inside the cottage it was almost too dark to see the

71

woman's face. But her hands, which closed on his, were ice cold.

"What's wrong, Marilyn?"

"I—I thought if I kept the lights off no one would know whether I was home or not."

"Your car's out back. I noticed it."

"I could have walked somewhere in the village."

"Well, my Jeep is out front now, so people will know you've got a caller."

"I suppose—" She moved away from him and a light switch clicked. The pleasant little living room was lighted by three lamps that came on simultaneously from the switch. Uncle George was shocked by the haggard look of Marilyn's face. It had been a bad day for her—the death of a friend—but not enough to account for what he interpreted as stark terror. He saw that shades and curtains were drawn over all the windows.

"I came as soon as I got your message," he said. "What is it? Something about Paul Comargo?"

She nodded, moved across the room to her desk, took something out of a drawer.

"The RFD man delivers the mail here about one in the afternoon," she said. "I don't get home from school till about three-thirty. Today it was later. The whole school was in turmoil, as you can imagine. When I got to my mailbox out front there was the usual junk mail, a couple of bills, a letter from an old friend who's living in California— and this."

She held out what she had taken from the desk drawer to Uncle George. He saw at once that it was a piece of plastic tubing about a foot long. Wrapped around it was a piece of paper held in place by a rubber band.

He knew, even as he slipped off the rubber band and unfolded the paper that the piece of tubing was exactly like the material that had been inserted in Paul Comargo's living grave. There was a message typed on the paper.

72

You have already stuck your neck out too far. Go
any further and there will be a longer piece of this
tubing attached to the box in which you'll be
buried.

"You—you understand why I asked you to come,
George," Marilyn said.

He felt an unaccustomed chill run along his spine. Late
in the morning he had talked with Marilyn at the school.
Someone had watched, knew, and left this grim warning
for her. But almost certainly this killer or killers had not
been watching Marilyn until he had made contact with her.
He was the one who was being watched! Someone out
there in the early evening shadows knew he was here,
knew that Marilyn was keeping in touch with him, must
know that he'd spent time at Hilltop and probably guessed
that he was flirting with the truth about Anne Hopkins. It
could be someone he knew, someone he passed the time of
day with at the post office, at the supermarket. It could be
someone he called "friend." It was someone who knew the
town, the people, who had gone terror-crazy.

As a prosecuting attorney George Crowder had never
felt any qualms about taking on a criminal with the ordinary
motives—greed, jealousy, revenge—but the psycho was
something else again. What drove him to violence was
never clear; there was never an established pattern you
could look for.

"Is there something you didn't tell me this morning,
Marilyn?" he asked. "You stuck your neck out by putting
me on the trail of Paul Comargo. But what other information do you have that would make this crazy warn you?"

Marilyn shook her head, slowly. "I—I told you everything there is to tell, George. I was a message service for
Anne—no more than that. The only thing Anne ever told
me about her Paul was that she felt certain her stepfather
was hounding him. Nothing else. Nothing about him or his

73

family or any other details about him. I never saw him. I wouldn't have known him if I passed him on the street."

"Nothing that could be dangerous to the killer?"

"Nothing!" And then her eyes widened. "Unless Lucius Hopkins, who certainly knew I was close to Anne, thinks she may have told me something that would harm him. She didn't, beyond telling me that he was a stern, maybe a vengeful, man."

"You picture Lucius Hopkins burying a man alive and letting him die?" Uncle George asked. "You picture him arranging for the violent death of his wife's daughter?"

"George, I can't picture anyone as being capable of doing either of those things," Marilyn said.

"And yet someone has, and left you a warning message of a pretty grim sort. If the warning was meant for you, Marilyn."

"It was in—my mailbox."

"The minute you found it you could be counted on to do one of two things," Uncle George said. "You would come to me for advice and help, or you would go to the State Police. In either case the whole community would be warned that the killer is still in Lakeview, ready to strike again in his own special way. Whoever he meant to warn—you, me, someone we don't even know about—would get the message."

"But it was in my mailbox!"

"And you want protection."

"Oh, my God, George, do I?"

"You have friends who would put you up for the night or come and stay with you here?"

"I can't ask friends to run that kind of risk for me, George."

"Could get hurt if someone is taking aim at you?"

"Of course!"

"Every cop, sheriff, deputy, state trooper is working overtime on Comargo's murder," Uncle George said. "It would be pretty hard to get one of them assigned to sit on your front porch all night."

"When a citizen has been threatened?"

Uncle George was silent for a moment, frowning. Then he pointed to the piece of tubing and the note that had been wrapped around it. "Could this be some kind of vicious practical joke played on you by some student at the school who has a grudge against you? Typewriters there, every kid in town knows the details of the Comargo case. My nephew Joey had the gruesome details for all your student body. You can buy this kind of tubing in a hardware store or pick up a piece of it in a garage."

"You don't really think that's possible, do you, George?"

"Kids saw me at the school talking to you this morning. That would tie you into the case, they'd think."

"Do you really think that's possible?"

He put his hand on the frightened woman's shoulder. "No, I don't really, Marilyn. But it's a terrible thing that's going on in our world today. I call it the 'copycat syndrome.' Someone commits an act of terrorism with some kind of an understandable motive—Arab against Jew, Irish against English, communist against military dictatorship—and instantly some psycho without any motive at all except to satisfy a hunger for violence, for notoriety, copies the crime. A year ago a man was buried alive in Texas, exactly the same way Paul Comargo was buried. It was described in every newspaper, on every radio and TV network. That man was lucky enough to be rescued alive. Paul Comargo, God help me, missed surviving by minutes. If I'd come back from Pennsylvania a day earlier Timmy would have found him and I would have saved him. The copycat aspect of it remains, down to the last nail driven into the coffin to torture the victim. If someone wanted to torture Paul Comargo why choose this elaborate pattern? Because it would attract attention, warn someone else."

"Warn who?" Marilyn asked. "Why me? I don't know

anything that would point to anyone, put anyone in danger!"

"I don't know," Uncle George said. "It may have been a way to warn someone else not so easy to get to." He found himself thinking of the locked gates at Hilltop. "It could be a way to terrorize a whole town. When this gets out, when the question spreads about Anne Hopkins's death, there'll be fear in every heart and mind in Lakeview. A maniac on the loose, ready to strike at anyone for no reason at all."

"You think that's what it is?"

"Not really, Marilyn."

"Damn you, George!" Hysteria was mounting in her. "You keep suggesting things and then admitting you don't believe them."

"It's a kind of process of elimination, girl," he said. "Along the way I'll come up with something I can't shake off."

One thing was certain. Marilyn couldn't be left alone here in her cottage. The ugly threat left in her mailbox had her very close to a crackup. She was persistent in refusing to ask friends to give her shelter or to ask someone to come there to stay with her. You don't ask friends to run that kind of risk for you.

Uncle George tried to reach Red Egan, but all he got on the sheriff's phone was an answering service: "This is Red Egan. I'm not in my office at the moment. When you hear the buzzer signal please leave me your name and a phone number where you can be reached."

"We've got to show your little present to the State Police," Uncle George told Marilyn. "Pack yourself an overnight bag, and we'll find you someplace safe to spend the night."

Captain Purdy sounded crisp on the phone. "You got a new twist to your soap opera, George?"

"This one is for real," Uncle George told him. "Marilyn

76

Stroud has received a threat. I'm bringing her over to see you."

"Your New York Homicide friend is here, just about to leave for the city," Purdy said.

"Tell him to hang on. I'll be there in about ten minutes."

Lakeview was not its normal self that evening. Lights, inside and outside houses, were everywhere. Two State Police cars, lights flashing on their rooftops, were methodically patrolling the village. Marilyn, almost ghostly pale, drove her own car to the barracks, with Uncle George following directly behind her in his Jeep. He had put the piece of plastic tubing and threatening note in a piece of kitchen foil and had it in the pocket of his parka. If Marilyn was being watched there was no way to conceal her journey to the barracks. She was sticking her neck out again, but there was no choice.

Captain Purdy had had a long hard day, and it showed on his face; dark circles under his eyes, lines etched deeper at the corner of his mouth. Lieutenant Kreevich looked fresh and relaxed as a man on a holiday. Uncle George knew from experience that Mark Kreevich thrived on action.

Marilyn explained what Uncle George put down on Purdy's desk.

"Something I hadn't told you before," Uncle George said. "It was through Marilyn that I got onto Paul Comargo. At the time there seemed no reason to make her a target for Lucius Hopkins. All we needed was to identify the dead man."

"How long have you been Anne's message service?" Purdy asked the girl.

"Fourteen, fifteen months," Marilyn said.

"How would anyone know?"

"No way, unless Anne told someone. George came to see me early at the school this morning. If they were watching him—"

"What put you onto Marilyn, George?"

"My sister knew that Marilyn was close to Anne, helped her get her job at the school. Anne had told us there was someone here in town taking messages for her. Marilyn seemed like a number-one choice. It paid off."

"May I ask a question, Captain?" Kreevich asked.

"Shoot the works, Lieutenant."

"You found this tubing and the note in your mailbox, Miss Stroud. About what time?"

"A little after four."

"And the RFD man delivers the mail at—"

"About one-thirty."

Kreevich glanced at Purdy. "The mailman would know whether this tubing and the note was in Miss Stroud's box when he delivered."

"Might, might not," Purdy said. "He picks up and delivers at more than a hundred boxes."

"So if this stuff was in the box he'd have picked it up to see if it was something to go," Kreevich said. "It would have been unusual enough for him to remember it, wouldn't you think?"

"I suppose."

"If it was put there after he delivered, then it had to have been done in broad daylight. Someone may have seen somebody monkeying around Miss Stroud's mailbox."

"It's worth a try," Purdy said. He picked up the phone and asked his switchboard to locate Fred Smith, the local RFD man.

"It shouldn't be too hard for your lab to decide whether this piece of tubing is a match for the one used in Comargo's box," Kreevich said. "And the typewritten note; typewriters are as individual as fingerprints, Captain."

"Hundreds of typewriters in town," Purdy said.

Kreevich smiled at him. "Nothing that pays off ever comes easy, Captain."

"Right now we have to arrange some protection for Mari-

lyn," Uncle George said. "I don't suppose you have someone you can assign to spend the night at her cottage with
her."

"Every man in my command is on duty, combing this
town for God knows what," Purdy said, sounding angry.
"Red Egan and all his deputies the same."

Kreevich's smile was cheerful. "You ever spend a night
in jail, Miss Stroud?" he asked.

"No!"

"I expect the captain could find you a nice clean cell—
keep the door unlocked, of course. It would take an army to
get at you in here, Miss Stroud.

"It's the best I can do for you, Marilyn," Purdy said.
"Every man I've got is out on patrol."

"I suspect the captain might even find a radio for you to
keep you entertained," Kreevich said. His hand was resting
on the portable radio on Purdy's desk.

Purdy seemed to relax a little. "I believe I could," he
said.

"We'd all feel better about you, Marilyn," Uncle George
said. "In the morning we can make some kind of regular
arrangement to look out for you."

Marilyn looked from one to the other of the three men.
"If—if you think I should—"

"Good girl," Uncle George said.

Uncle George and Kreevich were left alone when Purdy
led Marilyn out of his office. Kreevich's easy manner
seemed to tighten.

"Sorry I've got to go back to the city, George. Maybe I
can be of some help down there, though."

"I've got a feeling it's all right here somewhere," Uncle
George said.

"Looks like it," Kreevich said. "But Greg Lewis and I
may be useful."

"Where is Lewis, by the way?"

"Took the late-afternoon bus back to the city," Kreevich said. "Works a night shift down there. Incidentally, George, Purdy gave me an idea of how you're thinking about Anne Hopkins. I've got to tell you it feels hotter than anything else I've heard. Why do you suppose Purdy shies away from it?"

"Hopkins is the kind of man who can throw a lot of weight around," Uncle George said. "You don't mess around with him or his family unless you want to feel the heat."

"You've been messing around with him, according to Purdy."

Uncle George grinned at his friend. "Maybe I'm heat-proof," he said. "I don't have a job I can lose. I quit long ago."

"That's where I may be able to help you—the lost-jobs department," Kreevich said. "Who twisted whose arm to get Paul Comargo kicked out of college and fired from three or four jobs? I think I can apply a little official heat of my own to get some answers to that. If it comes up Hopkins right down the line we may be able to soften him up a little. I'll stay in touch, George. If I don't report in pretty quickly I may be out of work myself."

It was about eight o'clock when Uncle George drove his Jeep up the logging road to his cabin. It was his intention to pick up his dog, Timmy, Anne Hopkins's nightgown, and go out to cover the road between the hospital and Hilltop. Timmy wouldn't need daylight to pick up a trail if there was one.

But there was no Timmy waiting for him at the cabin, nor was he inside. Nor was Joey still there. Within a few seconds the whole story was there for Uncle George to read. Joey and Timmy were both gone, Anne Hopkins's crumpled up nightgown was gone, and a rifle was missing from the gun rack at the far end of the room. Dr. Watson had decided to help out Sherlock Holmes with a little snooping of his own.

"Damn fool kid!" Uncle George muttered.

Hopefully, the boy had gone home by now, taking Timmy with him. The dog, so completely Uncle George's, would go with the boy because he considered him family. One thing was certain, Timmy would not be inside the Trimble's house if Hector Trimble was anywhere about. He wasn't waiting outside the house on the main street of the village when Uncle George arrived there a few minutes later.

It was Hector Trimble who opened the front door to Uncle George's knock, his eyes glittering behind his steel-rimmed spectacles.

"About time!" he said. He looked past his caller out into the night. "Where is he?"

"That's what I came to ask you," Uncle George said. He saw his sister, Esther, standing just beyond in the living room. He guessed she'd been given a bad time by Hector about Joey and his "disreputable uncle."

"He didn't come home for supper, George, and we haven't heard anything from him," Esther said.

"It's rather complicated to explain, Es," Uncle George said. "I think something may have happened to Anne Hopkins last night somewhere between the hospital and Hilltop. I got a piece of Anne's clothing and I planned to go out there, with Timmy, to see if we could come across anything. When I got home Joey was there—about four-thirty. You sent him, Hector, with a message from Marilyn Stroud."

"Marilyn said it was urgent," Hector said. "I had to send someone."

"Well, I told Joey what I was planning to do—use Timmy to find some trace of what had happened last night. But I thought I better get to Marilyn first."

"Is she all right, George?" Esther asked.

"She's safe, if that's what you mean. I'm not going to take time now to tell you about it. I went to her, eventually took her to the barracks, spent time talking with Jim Purdy and Mark Kreevich. I got home twenty minutes ago. Timmy was gone, Joey was gone, the piece of Anne's clothing was gone, and a rifle out of my gun rack. Joey evidently thought he could help me while I was tied up with Marilyn's problem."

"You mean he's out in the woods somewhere, with a town full of maniacs?" Hector almost shouted.

"He's as good in the woods as anyone," Uncle George said. "He can handle a rifle and that dog as well as I can. I'll find him." He turned away.

"I knew damn well that, sooner or later, what you taught him would get him in big trouble. I'm going to call the sheriff."

"Don't bother," Uncle George said. "I'm stopping on the way to get him."

Lights were on in Red Egan's combination store and office when Uncle George got there. Red and a couple of his deputies had just come in from a stretch of patrolling the town. Uncle George told his story and the four men set out for the hospital in two cars, carrying flashlights and the sheriff and his deputies armed with rifles. At the hospital they split up and started to walk the mile and a half to Hilltop, Uncle George and Red Egan working one side of the road, the two deputies the other. They walked through the brush, a few yards in from the road, flashing their lights and calling out to Joey. Uncle George had a silent dog whistle which he knew Timmy would answer. He kept blowing it without results.

It was a painfully slow business with nothing to show for it. They'd gone almost a mile, Uncle George guessed, when one of the deputies from the other side of the road called out.

"Over here! Red! George!"

Uncle George and Red raced across the road to where they could see the deputies' flashlights blinking. One of the men came toward them.

"He's hurt bad," the deputy said.

Uncle George plowed ahead to where the other deputy was kneeling, his flashlight aimed at the ground. My God, Joey!

But it wasn't Joey. Lying in the grass, whimpering feebly, was Timmy, the setter. He was smeared with blood, a gaping wound in one shoulder, an ear hanging by what looked like a thread, a front leg mangled.

"Looks like a bear chewed him up," the kneeling deputy said.

Uncle George was down on the grass beside his dog.

"It's all right, boy," he said softly, his face close to the dog's bloody head. Timmy's tongue gave his master's face a tentative lick.

"No sign of Joey?" Red Egan asked.

"The dog was whimpering. We heard him. But no sign of the boy. If he got caught in the same meat grinder—?" The deputy shrugged.

# Part_____
## TWO

# 1

Uncle George had taken off his parka and wrapped it around the wounded Timmy.

"Got to get him to Doc Andrews," he heard himself say. "He's lost a lot of blood." And yet he couldn't move. Joey must be somewhere nearby.

"Probably scared off by whatever attacked the dog," Red Egan said.

"Joey doesn't scare easily," Uncle George said. "He has a rifle and he can handle it as well as you or I could. If some animal attacked Timmy while Joey was around he'd have shot it dead—and he'd be here caring for the dog."

"Maybe he went somewhere for help," Red Egan said. "The dog would have been a little much for him to carry a mile down the road."

"We'd have passed him—all the time shouting for him."

"So if he's hurt, too—"

The two friends stared at each other in the glow from a flashlight. The night was pitch dark, moon and stars clouded over. There were hundreds of acres of dense woodland on both sides of the road. Joey wouldn't be lost in those woods. They'd been his playground since he was a very small boy. But hurt and unable to answer their calls to him, they'd be lucky to stumble on him. It could take hours, even days, to cover the whole territory.

"I know you don't want to leave here, George," Red Egan said. "If you'll trust me I'll carry the dog back to my car and get him to Doc Andrews. I'll round up some more guys and we can launch some kind of organized search for the boy."

"Thanks, Red."

"Here, take my coat. You'll need it. I'll stay warm carrying the dog and there's a heater in my car. I should be back inside an hour. Take a little time to organize an army."

"Thanks again, Red." Uncle George bent down to the dog he was holding in his lap. "Take it easy, boy. It's going to be all right."

The dog whimpered as Red Egan lifted him up. "Be back as quick as I can," the sheriff said.

Uncle George and the two deputies listened to Red make his way out to the road. One of the men, without consultation, walked away into the woods, calling out Joey's name. The other, Frank Paxton, who was a boyhood friend of Uncle George's, kept flashing his torch around the area where they'd found Timmy.

"No sign of any kind of a fight right around here, George," Paxton said. "Looks to me like the dog crawled here after he was hurt. Could have been quite some distance."

"Joey?" Uncle George asked in a flat, cold voice. "A fight with an animal would have been noisy. Joey had a gun and he knows how to use it. He wouldn't have let Timmy be mangled the way he is."

"He and the dog could have got separated," Paxton said. "From what you told us, Joey would have given the dog that nightgown to smell. The dog has been trained to circulate, wider and wider, trying to pick up the trail. He and the boy could have wound up a long distance apart."

"You've heard a dog fight, Frank? It's a noisy business. It could be heard for miles out here in the quiet woods, at night."

"Maybe. Maybe it wasn't that noisy—a life-and-death struggle."

Uncle George looked down at Red's coat and saw that it, too, was stained with Timmy's blood. "The boy, trained to work with a hunting dog, wouldn't have strayed that far away from him, Frank."

"He was playing cops and robbers, not hunting," Paxton said. "Could have changed his way of acting. He could be on the other side of the road, a couple of miles from here, playing detective."

"I'd give an arm to believe that, Frank," Uncle George said.

And, God help him, he thought, his arm was safe. Joey and Timmy, doing what they were doing, would have worked like a team, never more than a few yards from each other. He knew because he had taught them. He had never wanted his hunting dog to be beyond a soft voice call.

It could be—it just could be—that playing a detective game Joey and the dog had separated. It could be—it just could be—that Timmy had encountered some wild animal. A raccoon could give a dog, even one as big as Timmy, a pretty good going over. At this time of year sometimes wilder game came down from the upper levels, looking for food. One of the deputies had mentioned a bear. There were always rumors about bears, although in all his years in Lakeview Uncle George had never seen one. Occasionally over the years a pack of wild dogs had invaded the community, feeding off cattle and sheep, and attacking fiercely anyone who stood in their path. But there'd been no talk of such a pack for several years.

Uncle George, standing there in the darkness, listening to the deputy crying out Joey's name in the distance, couldn't shake the conviction that if Joey was hurt or in trouble—he wouldn't let himself go beyond that. It was at the hands of someone—or some people—who had murdered twice in the last twenty-four hours, had left gruesome warnings in a mailbox, and was calmly watching every move that could be a threat. A small boy and a dog could have found something, some kind of evidence, and been stopped from getting away to report that finding. God help Joey if that was the case!

"Frank, if anyone has harmed that boy you're going to have to find me a lawyer," Uncle George said.

"He's just lost, George. We'll find him. But why a lawyer?" Paxton asked.

"Because I will commit a murder in the coldest blood, Frank."


Red Egan managed to round up about twenty men ready and willing to be part of a search for Joey Trimble. Most of them knew Uncle George and liked to think of him as a friend. Any of them who'd ever needed to buy an aspirin tablet knew Hector and Esther Trimble. And, as some wag said later, a boy is a boy is a boy, whether you know his family or not.

The search party arrived at the scene in a couple of vans and a pickup truck. Most of them carried rifles. There was the threat of some big beast who had ripped Timmy, a sturdy dog, apart, and in the back of most of their heads was the image of some monster who in the last hours had murdered two young people in their town. There was very little of the laughing and joking that can usually be heard when a group of young men get together on a project. They had to feel that they, themselves, were at risk.

The men stretched out in a line, working about ten feet apart, poking into every little thicket of brush or growth of weeds. Almost constantly someone was calling out Joey's name. If the boy was conscious and in this area he had to know that an army was looking for him.

As they worked their way up the hill on both sides of the road Uncle George felt a mounting tension. They were drawing close to the iron gates of Hilltop, the Hopkins estate. Any trail that Timmy and Joey might have picked up would, almost certainly he felt, lead to Hilltop.

It was no longer so dark in the woods bordering the road. A second rash of volunteers were appearing from town. Cars moved slowly, an effort being made to focus headlights on the area the men on foot were searching. A state-trooper car had joined the hunt and a swiveling searchlight on its roof darted from place to place, looking for a boy who must be badly hurt if he was in the area and didn't respond.

The Hopkins mansion on the hill above them was brightly lighted, and there were lights burning on either side of the closed iron gates. This was the end of the line without cooperation from Hopkins people. Sure enough, Joe Bradshaw, the night watchman, was standing just inside the gates, his boxer held tightly on a choke-chain leash.

"What the hell's going on?" he called out.

"Looking for a lost kid," Red Egan told him.

"No one's come inside," Bradshaw said. "Charlie would have let me know if they had."

Uncle George moved up close to the gate. "Mind if I have a look at your dog, Bradshaw?"

"Oh, it's you, Crowder. What do you want to look at Charlie for?"

"The missing kid had a dog with him that got badly chewed up," Red Egan said. "If he fought your dog there'll be some marks on him."

"I'd have heard a dog fight," Bradshaw said. "Charlie hasn't got a mark on him."

"Mind if I look?" Uncle George persisted.

"Go ahead, flash your lights on him," Bradshaw said.

Half a dozen torches focused on the dog who was snarling and tugging at his chain collar.

"He'll let me look," Uncle George said. "We made friends this morning, remember?"

"Don't try it, Crowder. He's a different dog at night,"

Bradshaw said. He moved the dog around in a circle. There didn't appear to be a scratch on him. He might have been too much for Timmy, but the setter wouldn't have rolled over and played dead in an encounter with him. The trooper car had pulled up and its searchlight focused steadily on the angry dog.

Red Egan turned to Uncle George. "Clean as a whistle, George," he said.

Two young men, complete strangers to Uncle George, joined them at the gate. Apparently their car had been blocked down the road by the searchers' vehicles.

"What's going on here?" one of them asked.

"Kid lost in the woods," they were told.

"We'd like to get into the Hopkins place," the young man said. "We're friends of Jerry Hopkins. He's expecting us."

"You got names?" Bradshaw asked them.

"Ed Girard," the young man said.

"Dave Lawrence," the other one said.

Bradshaw went into the gatehouse where there was obviously a phone, taking the boxer with him.

"Local kid?" the young man named Girard asked.

"My nephew," Uncle George said.

"All hell seems to have broken loose in this town," the one named Lawrence said. "Guy buried alive, then Jerry's sister, now your kid."

"We're here to help out the family with Anne's funeral," Girard said.

Bradshaw, the night watchman, came out of the gatehouse. "It's okay for you two to go in, if you can get your car through this mob."

"Thanks," Girard said. "I'll get the car, Dave."

Dave Lawrence reached his hand through the gate toward the boxer dog and almost got it taken off.

"You ought to know better than to try to pet a guard dog," Bradshaw said.

Lawrence looked a little sheepish. "He was friendly enough the last time I was here."

"You were inside then. That cleared you."

The searchers moved aside for the expensive sports car Girard brought up the road. Lawrence got in with him, Bradshaw opened the gates, and the two young men drove up the hill toward the big house. Uncle George, outside the now-closed gates, watched the car's taillights disappear around a bend in the road. He turned to Red Egan.

"Bradshaw live in town somewhere?" he asked, in a low voice the watchman couldn't overhear from the other side of the closed gates.

"No. He's an outsider; lives in a cottage there on the grounds."

"Joey can be in there, somewhere," Uncle George said.

"What makes you think so?"

"Trail would have led here, if Timmy and Joey found it," Uncle George said. "And the dog."

"What about him? He obviously didn't fight with Timmy."

"I'm not easily fooled by animals, Red. This morning I knew I could reach out for that boxer and he'd hold still for it. Tonight I knew just as surely that I couldn't."

"Not the same dog at night, he said."

"He's not the same dog. He's a totally different dog. He's got the same markings, could be out of the same litter, but he's not the same dog. I'll make you a bet the twin is in there with Timmy's teeth marks on him."

"So—we go in and search," Red said.

"I'm not sure I want to go in—openly," Uncle George said.

"Why?"

If they're holding Joey it could put him in danger if we look for him openly."

"Timmy got away."

"Could have slipped away, dragged himself to where we found him, while they were handling Joey."

"You got one shred of proof, we can get authority to search."

"So—there's nothing yet."

"Why would they be holding Joey?"

"Because he found out what happened to Anne and went too far with what he found."

"Then you can't wait, George!"

"They already know we're right on their doorstep, looking for Joey. It will take time to get a search warrant. Someone on the outside may know every step we take. If Joey knows something they can't let us know, they'll have plenty of time to silence him."

"What do you want us to do?" Red asked.

"Start the search going back toward the hospital, away from here. Back at my place I have a tranquilizer gun. Use it on wounded animals in the woods so we can help them when they're hurt. I'll come back with it and put that dog out of business while I search."

"What can I do?"

"Stay somewhere in this neighborhood, Red. If a car or cars start to leave from up there, make sure they aren't taking Joey somewhere. You've got the authority to stop and search. There's a killer on the loose."

"Do I tell Captain Purdy what you're thinking?"

"Just give me a little time on my own, Red. That boy means an awful lot to me."

In an emergency, time becomes a man's enemy. You can't, as a rule, stop to think up a plan if you want to rescue someone from a burning building. You have to act on your first impulse and carry it through, win or lose. There is, however, another kind of crisis, like the hostage situation in Iran which had lasted for more than a year. A wrong move could have resulted in mass execution. In that sort of setup you must take time to devise a plan that is foolproof.

Joey had been missing for four or five hours, assuming he had set out on his adventure shortly after Uncle George had gone to answer Marilyn Stroud's cry for help. Timmy, the setter, had escaped from his encounter—possibly a fight with a guard dog at Hilltop. Joey? If he had also been the victim of a violence it could very well be too late to save him. If he was being held prisoner by someone against whom he had discovered some kind of evidence, then a rescue plan must not be haphazard. Uncle George chose to believe that was the situation because the alternative, some kind of violent death for the boy, was unthinkable.

There was a chance, Uncle George told himself, that the boy was not in serious physical danger. He tried to put himself into Lucius Hopkins's way of thinking. Here was a man accustomed to power and to using it without regard to other people. He had bought himself an estate in a quiet country village where he had housed a fabulous art collection. In a lawless kind of society he had set up a system to guard against trespassers, vandals, and possible criminal assault—locked gates, fences, a night watchman, guard dogs. Suddenly there is a grisly murder of a young man to whom he'd been hostile, then the possibly nonaccidental death of his stepdaughter. The State Police, the local sheriff, and a local amateur crackpot named Crowder had invaded his privacy. When he had finally rid himself of those intrusions, a small boy and a dog had crept into the grounds, an unwarranted snooping. The guard dog had detected them, driven off the intruding dog in a vicious fight, while the boy was caught by Bradshaw, the night watchman, or someone else patrolling the grounds. Questioned, Joey would have identified himself as Hector Trimble's son and probably, proudly, claimed George Crowder as his uncle. It was time, Hopkins would tell himself, these local jerks were taught a lesson. The boy would be held and let the townspeople sweat it out for a while.

This was all a pure invention of Uncle George's, one he hoped might be true. He didn't want to look at the other side of the coin—that Lucius Hopkins was behind the murder of Paul Comargo, that he had faked the accidental death of his stepdaughter because she'd guessed the truth, that Joey, searching for some trace of what had really happened to Anne Hopkins, had come on evidence that had led him into the Hilltop grounds, been caught and silenced, just as Anne had been silenced. The dead boy's body could have been carried miles away in the trunk of a car, before the search had centered on Hilltop, and dumped where it would never be found.

That, too, was a pure invention of Uncle George's, but it had a frightening way of refusing to be rejected as too far-fetched and melodramatic. Just because a man wore a Brooks Brothers suit and drove a Rolls Royce didn't mean he wasn't capable of incredible violence.

But, Uncle George tried to reassure himself, there was a house full of people at Hilltop, the family, servants, guests. They couldn't all be psychotic. Or could they?

It was not a time to analyze the psychic quirks of the enemy. Joey was the thing. If he was at Hilltop it would take time to get a search warrant and barge in with cops, time enough to dispose of the boy if it had not already been done. The best chance was to slip in quietly, avoid the booby traps, and search.

One of the volunteer searchers who'd joined Red Egan's recruited force drove Uncle George back to the hospital where he'd left his Jeep when the original search for Joey on foot had started. There were claims on him in town but he told himself that Joey came first. His sister, Esther, would certainly understand that. How could he comfort her if he did stop by to see her? The old wheeze about "no news is good news" wouldn't do much to recharge her courage. He could imagine that her phone must be constantly ringing—ladies in town whose husbands or boyfriends were among the searchers, anxious to get possible news of what was happening out there in the woods. Esther would be the first to know, wouldn't she? It was her kid they were all looking for.

Uncle George drove by the drugstore and the Trimbles' lighted house, his head turned slightly away, his mouth a straight slit. He could almost hear Hector Trimble's harsh "I told you so." George Crowder would bring nothing but trouble to Joey, filling his head with storybook nonsense. Uncle George wasn't to know till later how Esther had answered her husband.

"Joey has a gun, Hector, and George has taught him how to use it. Thanks to George he may not be helpless."

"Damn-fool kid, trying to compete with the State Police!"

That's how it was going behind the lighted windows of the Trimble house.

The other claim on Uncle George was in young Dr. Tom Andrews's veterinary hospital. Andrews might just be able to tell him something useful, settle once and for all whether Timmy had been mauled by some kind of wild animal or in a fight with another dog.

The young vet was cleaning up what he called his operating room when Uncle George walked in.

"He's pretty badly beaten up, George," Andrews said.

"Guys up in the woods are talking about bears and wildcats," Uncle George said.

"I'd say it was almost certainly a dog, but one that was a little too much for Timmy."

"Can I see him?"

"I've got him sedated," the vet said. "He won't know you're here. I had to sew his ear back on. It was damn near ripped off. Shoulder wound is a mess, but not serious. Front leg chewed on like it had been a meal! I've given him antibiotics and a rabies shot, just in case. With luck, he'll come around in a few weeks."

"Thanks, Doc."

"You don't know who he fought with?"

"I have a theory."

"One thing I didn't mention," young Andrews said. "Timmy has two teeth broken off. I had to file them down to keep them from scraping the inside of his mouth. Looks like he might have clamped down very hard on something—like a chain collar."

"That fits."

"Like the guard dog at Hilltop?"

Uncle George nodded. "Except he doesn't have a mark on him. You happen to know if Bradshaw has two boxers?"

"Jake Wilson could tell you. He's there all day, every day. Bradshaw couldn't keep a second dog hidden away from him."

"It's funny," Uncle George said, "but I didn't see Jake among the people who came out to search for Joey and Timmy."

"You'll have to forgive me, but I haven't asked you about the boy, George."

"Still missing."

"I'm sorry. What was he doing up there in the woods on a cold night?" Andrews asked.

Uncle George's eyes narrowed. "Trying to find out what really happened to Anne Hopkins."

"You mean it wasn't a swan dive into an empty pool, the way they say?"

"I may be the only person around who thinks it wasn't. I've got a question for you, Doc. I've got a tranquilizer gun; use it on deer we find hung up in the woods. Knocks 'em out while we see if there's anything we can do to get them out of trouble. If I use it on a guard dog—any permanent damage?"

"Knock him out for about fifteen minutes. That's all."

"And if he comes to before I'm ready for him, what about a second shot?"

"Another fifteen minutes and pretty damn groggy for quite a while," Andrews said. "You think the boy may be inside the Hilltop grounds?"

"I don't think anyone who wishes him well is looking for him in there," Uncle George said. His voice was grim. "If I don't turn up by daylight you can tell them I told you I was going in the back way, over Hilltop Mountain. But before that, I told you nothing."

"Good God, George, you think—"

"I think you can only hang once, Doc, for a murder, or two murders, or three, or four. Once a man gets started killing it's like a roller-coaster ride. He just keeps going."

It isn't often that a man feels uncomfortable in his own home. There was something uneasy-making about the cabin as Uncle George approached it. There was no Timmy to greet him, no wide-eyed Joey asking for new stories of great adventure. Up the trail beyond the cabin there was an excavation that had been Paul Comargo's grave, a dark, smothering hole where that young man had fought desperately, hopelessly for his life.

There was no fire on the hearth and no reason to build one. This cold night was going to be spent searching outside for some clue to Joey's whereabouts. Uncle George went to a closet at the far end of the cabin's big living room. It was a large walk-in space where he kept outdoor equipment like fishing tackle, wading boots, such oddities as a bow and arrows, and the tranquilizer gun he'd mentioned to Doc Andrews. It was an awkward-looking weapon, resembling an antique long-barreled pistol. It was built on the principle of an air rifle, firing a needle-sharp pellet which, at reasonably close range, could penetrate the hide of an elephant. On a shelf was a cardboard box containing a supply of those tranquilizing pellets. Uncle George loaded the weapon with one of them and slipped two or three others into the pocket of his coat. It was only when he reached into the pocket of that coat that he realized that it was Red Egan's and not his own. A package of Red's inevitable cigarettes and a collection of kitchen matches was reminder enough. His own parka was probably back at Doc Andrews's place. It had been wrapped around Timmy when Red had taken the dog into the vets. In the pocket of that parka had been Uncle George's own pipe, pouch, and lighter.

Back at the gun rack across the way, Uncle George hesitated. There were half a dozen rifles and shotguns, weapons that Uncle George could handle in his sleep. It would, however, be awkward to carry one of them and the tranquilizer weapon. He opened a drawer at the bottom of the gun rack, unfolded a piece of yellow flannel, and took out a police special handgun. He checked the loading and slipped the gun into the pocket of his inner jacket. He didn't like handguns. They were for killing people, but, he told himself grimly, he was heading into murder country.

"Just hang tight, boy," he said out loud to a missing twelve-year-old.

The Crowder cabin and Hilltop, the Hopkins estate, were on the same side of the valley in which the town of Lakeview was located. Uncle George walked up the trail past the hole in the ground that had contained a coffin hours ago. He really didn't need the electric torch he'd brought along. He knew these woods like the back of his hand. There was a half-mile climb, another mile along a ridge, and he came to the boundaries of the Hilltop property. A glance at his watch told him that it was nearly midnight. Another mile away, at the top of the hill, he could see the lights from the Hilltop house. Some of the Hopkins family were obviously still up and about.

If Joey had come into the Hilltop grounds from the road below he wasn't likely to have been exploring this upper end of the property. Uncle George began moving slowly and quietly down the slope. He'd covered perhaps a hundred yards when he was brought to a stop by the low, snarling growl of a dog. He adjusted the tranquilizer gun to the ready and waited. The growl had turned into a kind of whimper, only a few yards away in the darkness. There was something wrong about this, he sensed. These were not the normal warning sounds you'd expect from an attack dog.

Uncle George took the electric torch out of his pocket, holding it in his left hand and the tranquilizer in his right. He switched on the torch. Almost instantly the light was reflected in the eyes of the big boxer. The growling was deeper in the dog's throat, but the animal didn't move from where he crouched in the grass. He should be in the air, Uncle George thought, aimed at this intruder's throat.

A movement of the torch revealed that the dog was stationed by what looked, for a moment, like a pile of rags. Uncle George took a step forward. The dog didn't move, the growling ceased. It was almost as if the dog was saying it was all right to come on. Another step forward and then Uncle George saw that the "pile of rags" was the body of a man. Someone of Red Egan's search party brought down by the killer dog, he thought.

Another two steps forward and still the dog didn't move. Almost before his torch revealed the truth Uncle George suddenly thought he understood the dog's behavior. The body in the grass was a friend of the dog's, not someone he'd brought down in an attack. Then the torch showed the mackinaw jacket Uncle George remembered that Bradshaw, the night watchman, had been wearing earlier. This was the dog's trainer, owner, master.

"Easy, boy," Uncle George said, and was standing beside the body. The dog was, literally, asking for help! He knelt down and knew, without touching the man, that there was no help he could give. The back of Joe Bradshaw's head had been smashed in as if it had been run over by a truck.

Suddenly there was light all around.

"Don't move an inch, Crowder, before you drop that gun," a cold voice said, "or I'll blow you into the next county."

## 2

Uncle George instantly knew who had spoken. It was Jerry Hopkins. He put the tranquilizer down in the grass and straightened up. Instantly someone came at him from behind and gave him a rough frisking. The handgun in his inside pocket was discovered and removed.

Blinded by flashlights, Uncle George realized that there were two or three of them. Jerry and his two young friends who had come for Anne's funeral? One of them had picked up the tranquilizer.

"Cockeyed kind of a gun," he said. He was the one who had called himself Ed Girard.

"So, now, Crowder, start walking toward the house," Jerry Hopkins said. "What's sticking in your back is a rifle. It can blow a hole in you big enough to drive a bus through. So, move."

Uncle George stood perfectly still. "You going to leave Bradshaw here?" he asked.

"Till the cops have a look and find out how you did it," Jerry said. "You stay here with him, Dave."

102

"If you take the dog with you," the one named Dave Lawrence said.

"There must be a chain collar in Bradshaw's pocket," Jerry said.

"You get it," Lawrence said.

"I won't go near the sonofabitch," Jerry said.

"I'll handle the dog for you, if you like," Uncle George said.

Jerry laughed. "That's how you got to Bradshaw, isn't it? You can handle the dog!"

"I can handle the dog because he's lost his anchor, his base of security," Uncle George said. There was a leash and choke collar protruding from Bradshaw's mackinaw pocket. "Easy, boy." Uncle George bent down, took the collar and leash from its place, spoke again to the dog, and slipped the choke collar over his head. The troubled animal seemed almost to show his relief. Authority he understood was in control again. "All right, boy, heel!"

The dog moved over to Uncle George's left side and stood at attention.

"You want to take him to the house, or to Bradshaw's cottage?" Uncle George asked.

"We pass the cottage on the way," Jerry said. "Get going, Crowder." The rifle was jammed hard into Uncle George's back. He didn't move.

"What are you three boys doing out here in the middle of the night?" he asked.

Jerry Hopkins's laugh was harsh. "Kind of a joke," he said. "We're looking for a missing boy. Hoped to find him before the whole town started swarming over us. We didn't have to kill a man to do it, though."

"You know perfectly well I didn't kill Bradshaw," Uncle George said.

"We'll let the cops decide that," Jerry said. "Now you better move, Crowder. It isn't against the law to kill a man

103

you find trespassing on your property. My old man will decide just what's to be done with you."

Uncle George looked down at the boxer. "Walk, boy," he said.

The dog moved along quietly beside Uncle George, not tugging at all at the leash. It was downgrade all the way to the big house and the cottage behind it. Jerry Hopkins walked behind, rifle at his prisoner's back. Girard was evidently beside him. Nobody spoke.

"You find any trace of the boy?" Uncle George called back over his shoulder.

"We wouldn't be out here on a cold night if we had," Jerry Hopkins said.

"You hear someone attack Bradshaw?"

"We caught you red-handed. That's good enough, isn't it? He didn't have to make any sound when you slugged him from behind, did he?"

They approached the cottage where Bradshaw lived.

"We'll just shove that animal in the cottage and go on into the house," Jerry said. "Open the door, Ed."

Girard moved around in front into Uncle George's line of sight.

"I'd like to have a look at the other dog," Uncle George said. "He's probably in there, chewed up a little."

"There's no other dog," Jerry said.

"Oh, come on, Hopkins. My dog wouldn't have left the other dog unmarked. This one is evidently a second animal Bradshaw was training. He hasn't developed the killer instinct yet. That's why Bradshaw wouldn't let any of us near the gate earlier on. We'd all have seen he wasn't dangerous."

"He snapped at Dave when he tried to touch him," Girard said.

"Just the beginning of training," Uncle George said. "A yank on this choke collar startled him."

"Take the leash and put the dog in the cottage, Ed," Jerry said.

Girard hesitated.

"I'll put him in for you," Uncle George said. He lowered his hand to the dog. "It's all right, boy." He led the dog to the door of the cottage and opened it. He bent down, slipped the choke collar off the dog, and gave him a little shove through the door, tossing the leash and collar in behind him. Then he turned and faced Jerry. The rifle was suddenly pressed right against his heart. Jerry's face was only a blur in the lights from the house. "Let's get it over with," he said. "I've still got a boy to find."

"I should have let you have it out there where we found you," Jerry said. "Now, for the last time—"

"Just tell me where you want me to go," Uncle George said.

The two young men stood in the entrance hall of the big house, guns pointed at Uncle George, young Hopkins shouting for his father. The study door at the end of the hall opened and Lucius Hopkins appeared.

"Ed and Dave and I were out looking for that lost kid," Jerry said. "We found Crowder out there. He was armed. Bradshaw is dead, Dad."

"*What?*"

"He must have come on Crowder snooping around and Crowder was too much for him."

"You bastard!" Hopkins shouted at Uncle George. Then he turned stone cold. "Ed, be good enough to call the State Police. Phone in my study. And send for an ambulance."

"No point, Dad," Jerry said. "Brad's dead. The cops won't want him touched."

"How can you be sure he's dead?" Hopkins asked.

"Just by looking at what's left of his head," Jerry said.

Hopkins almost crouched, as though he was going to

spring. "Why did you have to kill him? You were trespassing. You knew that Brad was only doing his job."

"I never saw Bradshaw—alive, that is," Uncle George said.

"We caught him, bending over Brad," Jerry said. "Probably beat him to death to keep from alerting anyone by firing a shot."

Hopkins was breathing like an exhausted runner. "I promise you, Crowder, I'll be right behind you every step of the way to the gas chamber—or wherever they execute criminals in this state."

There was an interruption at that moment. Delia Hopkins came down the stairway from the second floor. She was wearing a wine-colored housecoat.

"What on earth is going on down here?" she asked, standing at the foot of the stairs. "Mr. Crowder!"

"He killed Brad," Jerry said.

The woman looked shocked, but she moved quickly to her husband's side. "Oh, Lucius, I'm so sorry."

For a moment Hopkins seemed to crack. He put his arms around his wife, holding her very close.

"You picked the wrong target, Crowder," Jerry said softly. He was standing right by Uncle George, rifle still pressed against his prisoner's side. "Brad was the son of Dad's closest friend. Like a second son to him, older brother to me. Worked in the corporation's offices in New York. Got sick. Dad brought him up here where he could work outdoors, get his health back. Like I said, you picked the wrong target. Dad'll never let you go for this."

Delia Hopkins had turned away from her husband. "Why don't you put down that gun, Jerry? Mr. Crowder won't go anywhere."

"You're damn right he won't," Jerry said, not moving.

"How did it happen, Mr. Crowder?" Delia Hopkins asked.

"I'm afraid I can't tell you that, Mrs. Hopkins," Uncle

George said. "I came across Bradshaw, already dead, his dog crouched beside him. I was just trying to see if anything could be done for him when Jerry and his friends took charge."

"The dog didn't—"

"He put the dog out of business with a tranquilizer gun he had," Jerry said.

"I had a tranquilizer," Uncle George admitted, "but I didn't use it."

"Turned the dog into a pet lamb," Jerry said.

"Nobody seems to be interested in facts, Mrs. Hopkins," Uncle George said. "I did come onto your property from the high ridge. I did have a tranquilizer in case the attack dog made trouble."

"You were looking for your lost nephew?" Delia Hopkins said.

"'Lost' is a handy word, Mrs. Hopkins. We've 'lost' Joey, but he isn't 'lost' if he's anywhere around here. He grew up in these woods, has hunted in them, fished in them, camped out in them. Would it surprise you, in view of the violence that's gone on here in Lakeview in the last twenty-four hours, that I came looking for Joey carrying a gun?"

"Did you shoot Joe Bradshaw, Mr. Crowder?" Delia asked.

"No. He wasn't shot."

"The coroner will tell us that," Jerry said. "Shot him and then smashed in his head to hide the fact."

"You and your friends were out hunting for the lost boy," Delia said. "Did you hear a shot?"

"We were probably a long distance from there when it happened," Jerry said. "There's a lot of territory to cover here, mom."

"But a gunshot?"

"Half the town is out here in the woods, carrying guns. If we heard it I guess we just supposed—"

The one called Ed Girard came out of the study. "Captain Purdy will be here in twenty minutes, a half hour," he said. "But they've notified a patrol car. He could be at the gate any minute now."

"Go down and let him in, Jerry," Hopkins said.

"I'm not going to let this creep slip away on us," Jerry said, jamming the barrel of his gun hard into Uncle George's back.

"Give me the rifle. He won't go anywhere," Hopkins said. "I promise you." His cold eyes were fixed on Uncle George. He reached out for the rifle. "If you think I won't use it if you try anything, Crowder, you're very much mistaken."

"Don't worry, Hopkins," Uncle George said. "I'm as anxious as you are for the police to get here. Or do you really want them to come?"

"If you killed Brad I can't wait!" Hopkins said.

One thing was certain. Whoever the trooper was who was driving the patrol car he would be someone who knew Uncle George. Trooper Gus Arbetchian had been a part of the force at the barracks for several years. He knew the town and its people well. He looked to be slightly in shock when Jerry Hopkins brought him into the entrance hall where the elder Hopkins was holding a rifle on Uncle George.

"What the hell's going on here, George?" he asked.

"This man has killed Joe Bradshaw, my night watchman," Hopkins said. "We've been holding him till you got here."

"So, I'll take that rifle, Mr. Hopkins," Arbetchian said.

For just a moment it looked as if Hopkins would refuse, but then he backed away from Uncle George and handed the rifle to the trooper.

"Thanks, Gus," Uncle George said. "Hopkins seemed to have an awfully nervous trigger finger." He relaxed for the first time since the dog had growled at him at the north end of the property and he'd seen Bradshaw in the light from his torch.

"Like I told you, officer, my two friends and I, along with Bradshaw, were looking for that lost kid," Jerry said. "We heard the dog snarling. We hurried in the direction that came from and found Crowder bending over Brad. Dead as a mackerel. Head smashed in. The dog was quiet because Crowder had probably shot him with a tranquilizer gun he was carrying."

"George?" Arbetchian asked.

"No," Uncle George said.

"Handled the dog like it was his own pet," Jerry said. "Dave, my friend, is out with Bradshaw. He's got the tranquilizer. You can tell whether Crowder fired it."

"It's my job to keep things cool here till Captain Purdy shows up," Arbetchian said. He was showing the professional deadpan face that goes with a trooper on duty, but it was fairly clear that if he had to take sides it wouldn't be with the Hopkins entourage. Arbetchian, personally, had pulled in Jerry Hopkins for speeding, drunk driving, brawling in a local tavern, and seen him wriggle off the hook with the aid of his father's high-powered legal talent. That kind of thing had not endeared the young man and his family to the troopers. George Crowder commit a murder in cold blood? Never! But he had been trespassing on private property, legally posted. However, Arbetchian knew that Uncle George would break into the White House if it involved the safety of his beloved young nephew. Nor would the local court do more than slap him with a token fine if Hopkins insisted on his being charged. He was guilty of a technical violation which a decent man would forgive. The murder of a trusted employee could warp Hopkins's judgment, but to think for a moment that George Crowder was a killer was absurd. Arbetchian's thinking on the subject would be matched in hundreds of homes in Lakeview when the story broke. It was matched in the mind of Captain Purdy who arrived a few minutes later with half a dozen troopers, Dr. Walters, the local medical officer, and the paramedics from the local ambulance corps.

Jerry Hopkins told his version of the story.

"You do it, George?" Purdy asked.

"No."

"We better go have a look," Purdy said. "You better come along, George—tell us your side of it."

"You let him get away, Purdy, and so help me—" Lucius Hopkins's voice was shaking with anger.

"Where would he go, Mr. Hopkins?" the captain asked. "Everyone within a hundred miles knows him by sight. Let's get going. You lead the way, Jerry."

Uncle George had moved so that he was standing next to Delia Hopkins. "You find Anne's clothes?" he asked in a low voice.

The woman shook her head.

Flashlights blinked on the way up the hill to the scene of a death like a swarm of out-of-season fireflies. Uncle George, walking next to Captain Purdy, spoke quietly. "There's no way, I suppose, to keep this army from tramping out every possible clue there may be around the body."

Purdy nodded. About twenty yards away from where Dave Lawrence's light was focused on their approach, Purdy stopped and shouted an order to his men. "I want all of you to stay about twenty yards away from the body—Doc Walters, the stretcher-bearers, and George Crowder will go in with me. Stay away till I give the word."

"It's cops, Dave!" Jerry Hopkins called out. "It's okay!"

Young Dave Lawrence's face, illuminated by Purdy's torch, was the color of ashes. "I began to think no one would ever come." He held out Uncle George's tranquilizer gun. "This is what he used on the dog, I guess," he said.

Purdy took the tranquilizer weapon and turned his light on the firing mechanism. "It's not loaded," he said.

"The pellet he fired is in the grass over there where the dog was," Lawrence said. "I thought it was best not to touch it."

"You fire this thing, George?" Purdy asked.

"No."

"If you examine the dog—" Lawrence said.

Dr. Walters and the stretcher-bearers had moved in on Bradshaw's body. They could all hear the doctor's startled exclamation. "Holy God!"

"No question?" Purdy asked.

"No question," the doctor said. "Looks like he was hit a dozen times with your favorite 'blunt instrument.' Never made it after the first blow."

Uncle George was moving his torch around on the ground by the bloody remains of a man. "Not much to see here, Jim," he said to the captain. "Of course, there was young Hopkins, and his two friends, and me—and God knows who else. If you'll let the doc move the body out maybe you could fence this area off till daylight. Almost impossible to see anything important with these flashlights."

"The weapon," Purdy said.

"Could have been something like an iron wrecking bar," the doctor said, straightening up.

"Thrown away anywhere on this hillside," Uncle George said.

"Take him out, Jim?" the doctor asked.

"Go," Purdy said. He turned to Uncle George. "I'd better get the Hopkins story—and yours, George. I'll start my men looking for the weapon."

"There's a boy to be found, Jim," Uncle George said, his voice gone hard. "I want to keep looking."

"They've accused you of murder, George. I've got to have a statement from you. Half the town's looking for the boy."

"Not here, on this property," Uncle George said.

The doctor held out his hand. "Here's the pellet from that tranquilizer weapon, Jim."

Purdy looked at it and then at Uncle George. "It's been fired, George."

"Not by me."

"I think we better have your whole story, George."


Jerry Hopkins's story, supported by his two friends, seemed fairly straightforward when he made it, but that didn't happen until Captain Purdy had a head-on collision with the senior Hopkins.

Purdy had brought the three young men, Uncle George, and a trooper with a stenotype machine into Lucius Hopkins's study.

"You're not going to take Jerry's statement with this man Crowder present, are you?" Lucius Hopkins demanded.

"Why not?" the captain asked.

"Maybe you're not right in the head, Captain! Let Crowder hear what Jerry has to tell you and he can tailor his own story to fit."

Uncle George's smile was thin and tight. "He's right, you know, Jim. Why don't I tell my story first, and then Jerry can tailor his to fit mine?"

"I think Jerry has the right to have my lawyer present before he makes any kind of statement," Hopkins said.

"I'll be my own lawyer," Uncle George said. "This isn't any kind of sworn statement, Hopkins, that can be used in later proceedings. The captain just wants to know what

112

happened. Jerry and his two friends were together. They can support each other. I'll take my chances alone."

"We don't have anything to hide, Dad," Jerry Hopkins said.

"So tell me what happened," Purdy said.

It sounded perfectly reasonable as Jerry told it. Half the town had been outside the locked gates, looking for Joey. If they didn't find the boy pretty quickly a mob would be storming the Hilltop property. Inside the property they were all in pain, the shock of Anne's death. Jerry and his friends, with Bradshaw's help, had decided to comb the Hilltop grounds for the boy. If Joey Trimble was there somewhere and they could find him, they could avoid an invasion of strangers who would be prying into every nook and cranny of the place, possibly this main house itself.

"Save my mother more pain than she was already enduring," Jerry said.

The south side of the property bordered the road where the searchers were still milling around. It was decided that Ed Girard and Bradshaw would cover the west side of the land and work their way up to the north end. Jerry and David Lawrence would cover the east side and work their way up to the north where they'd meet the others.

"Bradshaw had his dog with him?" Purdy asked.

"Yes. On the leash. So many people around there was a chance he might attack a friend."

"So you hunted for the boy?"

"Sure. It's not wild country inside our fences, Captain. It's all mowed, cultivated, trimmed. No place for the boy to really hide except in the outbuildings—the bathhouse, the garage, the tool sheds where we keep a couple of tractors, the power mowers. Dave and I covered the barn and the toolsheds. I suppose Ed and Bradshaw covered the bathhouse, the cottage where Brad lived, the garage, right Ed?"

Girard nodded. "No sign of the kid there."

"And no sign of him in the barn or the tool sheds," Jerry said. "So then we started working our way up through the gardens, and toward the upper slope."

"You stayed together, you with Lawrence, and you, Girard, with Bradshaw?" Purdy asked.

"Brad and I split up, after we'd gone through the bathhouse and the cottage," Girard said. "Brad thought we'd cover more ground and faster if I followed the fence line and he headed straight up to the top."

"You and Lawrence stayed together, Jerry?"

"Yes, we did. The east side is the most cultivated. There's a grove of birch trees on the west side. I guess Brad thought he and the dog might have better luck where the growth was thick. If he and Ed split up they'd cover more ground in a hurry."

And so, according to Jerry, he and Lawrence and Girard eventually met at the top of the property.

"We looked down toward the birch grove for some sign of Brad's flashlight," Jerry said. "No sign of it or him. And then—then we heard the dog growling and snarling and we headed for that commotion."

"You called out to Bradshaw?"

Jerry hesitated. "I don't remember. We were running toward the sound the dog was making."

"It didn't sound very far away," Dave Lawrence said.

"Bradshaw wasn't shouting for help?"

"Then we saw a flashlight moving, focused down toward the ground," Jerry said. "The dog was still growling—kind of a warning sound, not the attack excitement. I made some kind of sign-language suggestion to Dave and Ed—we'd circle, come at whatever it was from three sides."

"You did that and moved in?" Purdy asked.

Jerry nodded. "In close I could see Brad lying there, on

the grass, the dog crouched beside him, and Crowder bending over him with what I thought was a rifle in one hand, flashlight in the other. I—I ordered him to drop the gun and we took him, searched him, found he was also carrying a handgun."

"A handgun and a rifle?" Purdy asked.

"I thought it was a rifle at first—odd-looking thing. Since then I've heard you call it a tranquilizer. Anyway, we brought Crowder down here to the house and phoned for you."

"You knew Bradshaw was dead?"

"Hell, man, you've just been looking at him. Did you need a medical opinion?"

"You say you brought George down here to the house and phoned for me, but actually Mr. Lawrence stayed with the body. Why?"

"Brad had obviously been murdered. That meant cops. I didn't want anything disturbed till you got here," Jerry said.

"Good thinking," Lucius Hopkins said.

"Make you nervous, Mr. Lawrence, staying up there alone with a dead man and a maniac running around loose?" Purdy asked.

Dave Lawrence gave Uncle George a quick look. "I guess I thought Jerry and Ed had taken the 'maniac' down here to the house," he said.

"The dog?" Purdy asked.

"Jerry and Ed and Crowder took the dog with them," Lawrence said. "Crowder handled that dog like he owned him."

"Had him tranquilized," Lucius Hopkins said, speaking for the second time.

"We put the dog in Brad's cottage and left him there," Jerry said. "Came here to the house and called you."

"None of you saw anyone moving around the property?" Purdy asked.

"Only Crowder," Jerry said. Girard and Lawrence both nodded in agreement.

Purdy turned to Uncle George. "You told me you didn't fire that tranquilizer gun at the dog, George."

"I didn't," Uncle George said.

Purdy turned back to Lawrence. "They left that tranquilizer with you, Mr. Lawrence. Did you fire it, maybe experimenting to see how it worked?"

"No!"

"It's made on the principle of an air rifle," Uncle George said. "It just makes a sort of 'ping' sound when it's fired. If he wasn't familiar with the sound Lawrence could have dropped it on the ground and not realized it had gone off."

"Did you drop it on the ground, Mr. Lawrence?"

"I—I don't know," Lawrence said. "I may have. I had my own rifle and I was keeping it at the ready—just in case."

"Just in case there was another 'maniac' around?" Uncle George asked. He was smiling.

"I—I suppose," Lawrence said.

Uncle George drew a deep breath. "Look, Jim, I've got a missing boy to find. So let's cut this short. Where I made contact with Jerry Hopkins and his friends their story is correct. They found me bending over Bradshaw, they disarmed me, we took the dog down to the cottage and they brought me here where they called you. I'm a supporting witness for all of that."

"They disarmed you—just like that?" Purdy asked.

"If you were holding a gun on me, Jim, I'd know you wouldn't fire unless I put up some kind of a fight. Three excitable young men are something else again."

"Specially when you'd murdered a trusted friend of theirs," Lucius Hopkins said, his anger still at a boiling point. "You came here with a weapon that would put the

116

dog out of business, you argued with Brad, and you killed him when he tried to warn you off the property!"

"Let me handle this, Mr. Hopkins," Purdy said.

"There's not much point in that, is there, Captain?" Hopkins said. "This man is your friend. You're on his side before you start!"

"So let me tell my friend my story and get it over with," Uncle George said. "Joey went hunting with my setter dog, Timmy, to find some kind of clue as to what really happened to Anne last night."

"A twelve-year-old boy?" Hopkins said, his laugh contemptuous.

"He knew that's what I intended to do, and when I was delayed by bringing Marilyn Stroud to you, Jim, he decided to try to help me. He came into this area and I tend to believe onto this property. The other dog chewed up Timmy, who got away. God knows what happened to Joey."

"What do you mean, 'other dog'?" Purdy asked.

"Maybe someone here will admit that Bradshaw had two boxer dogs, one fully trained as an attack killer, the other in the process of learning."

"That's crazy!" Jerry Hopkins said.

"The killer dog must have been marked up in the fight with Timmy. He's probably in the cottage, or hidden somewhere else. The second dog, the one who was up there when I found Bradshaw, could be handled because he hasn't been fully trained yet."

"What about that, Mr. Hopkins?" Purdy asked.

Hopkins hesitated, obviously trying to make up his mind to something. "All right, there *are* two dogs," he said.

"Dad!" Jerry's surprise was genuine, it seemed.

"Just a couple of weeks," Hopkins said. "Charlie, the original boxer, has come down with some sort of kidney failure. Brad knew he was going to have to have a new dog soon. Brad picked up this second dog at the place where he'd bought Charlie. He didn't want anyone to know there were two dogs until the new one was ready. Be an invitation to trespassers and snoopers. I don't know where Charlie is or whether he was in a fight, but Brad must have had the new dog with him tonight. Crowder could never have gotten within arm's length of Charlie."

"Thanks for that much truth, Mr. Hopkins," Uncle George said.

"Obviously you'd never have been able to attack Brad if Charlie had been with him," Hopkins said.

"And did you attack Bradshaw, George?" Purdy asked.

The urgent need to get looking for Joey was obviously getting to Uncle George. There was an edge to his voice. "Never saw him until the dog attracted my attention to him," he said. "Yes, I was trespassing, but the circumstances were unusual. Yes, I came to Hilltop with a tranquilizer, prepared to deal with the dog if I had to."

"You didn't ask for or expect any cooperation from the Hopkinses?" Purdy asked.

Uncle George hesitated, as if his legal mind was choosing his answer carefully. "There have been two violences connected with Hilltop in the last thirty-six hours," he said. "God forbid, there may have been a third involving Joey. Not everyone here at Hilltop would be in on this violence, but who would it be safe to ask for help?"

"I resent this kind of innuendo, Captain," Lucius Hopkins almost shouted. "A young man we knew in the most casual way was found buried alive—*on Crowder's property*, Captain! My daughter dies in an unfortunate accident—*after spending time with Crowder!* A boy and a dog—*Crowder's nephew and Crowder's dog*—suffer some mishap, possibly here at Hilltop. If it was here, they were trespassing. And who do we find bending over my murdered watchman and friend? *Crowder!* Crowder, admittedly trespassing, prepared to neutralize our perfectly normal defenses, putting our watchdog out of business. Stop favoring your friend here, Captain, and get on the ball!"

"I want this property searched from one end to the other," Uncle George said. "I want this house searched, the outbuildings searched, and as soon as it's daylight, every inch of the grounds."

"Over my dead body!" Lucius Hopkins countered. "Not without a court order and my lawyer present to protect my rights."

"I think I know the law well enough, Jim, to know that you don't need a court order," Uncle George said to Purdy. "You have Bradshaw murdered here at Hilltop. You don't need a court order to search for the killer or any clues that may lead to him."

Captain Purdy nodded slowly. "Crowder's right, Mr. Hopkins. I don't need a court order. Let's begin with the cottage. There may be something there that will tell why Bradshaw was attacked."


From Uncle George's point of view the essential purpose of the search was to make certain that every single room was looked into, every closet, every possible hideaway corner from attic to basement. That went not only for the main house, but for the cottage where Bradshaw had lived, the bathhouse, the garage, the barns, the tool sheds—every possible place where a twelve-year-old boy could be held prisoner, or—not to be even thought of yet—his body hidden.

"The thing that really started to eat at me," Uncle George told Red Egan later in the day, "was the thought that we should be wondering about the 'copycat' aspects of this case. I had the nightmare feeling that we should be looking for a piece of plastic tubing sticking up in the grass somewhere on the grounds, or in the surrounding woods. Someone had tried to punish Comargo, presumably for

119

getting in the way. Joey could have gotten in the way and the same game could be played with him. Felt like my blood had turned to ice water."

The logical place for Captain Purdy to begin his investigation was the cottage where Bradshaw had lived. The dog, or both dogs, would be there; some clue as to what Bradshaw may have known that had made him a target for the killer.

"I want you to come along with us to the cottage, George," the captain said. "You may be able to handle the dogs so that we won't have to hurt them. And I want you along, too, Mr. Hopkins, so that you'll know I'm not giving George some kind of special treatment."

Hopkins turned to Jerry. "Call Logan Forsythe again, Jerry, and tell him I need him here on the double." Then to Purdy: "I'm entitled to have my lawyer on the job."

Three troopers were left behind to search the house under the guidance of Hilda Clarkson, the maid, who had been summoned from her quarters. Captain Purdy, Trooper Arbetchian, Uncle George and Lucius Hopkins headed across the back garden to Bradshaw's cottage. It was dark, as it had been when Uncle George and Jerry and his friend, Ed Girard, had delivered the dog there earlier.

"You think you can handle that dog, George?" Purdy asked, fingering the butt of his holstered revolver.

"I can handle one of them," Uncle George said.

"There's a light switch just inside the door—to the right," Lucius Hopkins said.

Uncle George knocked gently on the door, and then turned the knob and opened it an inch or two. There was an instant low growl from inside.

"It's okay, boy," Uncle George said. "Friends!" He reached around inside, found the light switch, and the interior was flooded with light.

The dog was lying just inside the door, head lowered on

120

his front paws. He identified Uncle George and his stub of a tail wriggled slightly.

"What a good dog," Uncle George crooned at the animal and opened the door wide.

"What the hell!" Lucius Hopkins said.

Uncle George, who had knelt beside the dog to stroke his head, looked up. The inside of Bradshaw's cottage looked as if a tornado had struck it. Furniture was overturned, seat cushions of the chairs cut and ripped open, drawers from the sideboard taken out and the contents dumped on the floor, rugs rolled aside and pushed into a corner.

"The other dog," Purdy said.

"If he's here he should be sounding off," Hopkins said. The dog with Uncle George whimpered, pulled himself up and moved, stiff-legged, toward a door at the far end of the room.

"The kitchen," Hopkins said. "God Almighty, what struck this place?"

Uncle George followed the dog to the far door, opened it onto darkness. He raised his hand for silence. Purdy, just behind him, had drawn his gun. There wasn't a sound from the dark room beyond. Uncle George reached for where a light switch might be and found it. The kitchen had been hit by the same frantic signs of a search as the living room. That wasn't, however, what held Uncle George riveted where he stood in the doorway.

"Put your gun away, Jim—you don't have to worry about the other dog," he said.

The second boxer dog lay on the floor in a pool of blood.

"Jesus!" Purdy said. "Somebody cut his throat!"

Trooper Arbetchian wedged past Uncle George into the room and bent down by the dog. "He's got other wounds," he said, "but his throat's been slit from ear to ear. Blood's still wet."

"There's a knife over there by that upset table," Purdy said. "Handle it with care, Arby. Fingerprints."

"That other damned dog let it happen!" Hopkins said. He sounded more stunned now than angry.

"That's not the way I read it," Uncle George said.

## 3

"I don't know too much about this second dog," Uncle George said. "Don't know his name. I suppose we could call him Charlie Two. He isn't fully trained, but I don't think he would have stood by without some kind of outcry while this cottage was turned upside down and the other dog killed. You'd have heard him in the house. I think Charlie Two can help us put this together, at least as to timing."

"I'm not following you, George," Purdy said.

"I found Bradshaw up at the north end of the property, dead, with Charlie Two lying beside him, growling, warning. He wasn't on the leash. The leash was in Bradshaw's pocket. We took it to bring Charlie Two down here—Jerry, Girard and I. When we got here I opened the front door, took the leash off the dog, pushed him in, and tossed the leash in after him. It's just inside the front door now where I threw it."

"Which spells what?" Purdy asked.

"Bradshaw had gone with Jerry and his friends to look for Joey." A nerve twitched high up on Uncle George's cheek. Just the mention of Joey was painful. "Bradshaw separated from Dave Lawrence with whom he was searching, taking the dog with him—not on the leash. He and the dog must have separated as they worked their way up through that birch grove someone mentioned. At the top of the property Bradshaw encountered his killer. There's no way to guess yet what happened between them, but it couldn't have been noisy. Jerry and Ed Girard weren't far away, according to them. Bradshaw was killed. It could have only been a moment later that the dog found him, crouched beside him to protect him. And then I came on them, working my way down from my property."

"The dog didn't try to attack you?"

"I think he knew his master needed help," Uncle George said.

"And the killer?"

"He must have come down here before I found Bradshaw," Uncle George said. "He was obviously looking for something terribly important to him. Charlie One was here, made some move to attack, and got his throat cut."

"And he was long gone before we got a call from the Hopkinses and arrived," Purdy said.

"Gone from here, at any rate," Uncle George said.

"This is all a dream-up, isn't it?" Lucius Hopkins said.

"Add up the facts we have some other way, Hopkins," Uncle George suggested.

"I need my fingerprint people to go over this place," Purdy said. "Get 'em here, Arby. Every damn thing in here has been handled. There has to be something for us."

Arbetchian took off.

"Now, Mr. Hopkins, I need some kind of a briefing from you on Bradshaw," Purdy said. "Who was he, his family, how he came to be working for you, who could have hated him with such a violence?"

Hopkins seemed to make an effort to pull himself together. "It's hard to imagine how anyone could hate a man so much," he said. "But when you think of that boy in the coffin, you know it has to be someone sick, sick, sick."

"And when you think of your daughter and my nephew," Uncle George said.

"You're still playing with the idea that Anne's death wasn't accidental, Crowder?"

"Still," Uncle George said. "And I still think my Joey may have found out the truth."

"About Bradshaw," Purdy said.

Hopkins glanced down at the dead dog and a little shudder shook him. "Can we get out of this damned blood bath?" he asked.

"We'd better go back across to the house when Arbetchian gets back. I don't want anyone touching anything in this place until the fingerprint people have given it a thorough going-over."

The three men moved out onto the little front porch of the cottage. The big house across the garden was brightly lighted from top to bottom. There must, Uncle George thought, be dozens of places to hide someone or something there. The Cranes must have built the house nearly a century ago. There could be attic closets, forgotten basement storerooms. He ought to be there, making sure that Purdy's men didn't miss a single crevice where Joey might be concealed. He glanced at his watch. Time had galloped on, it was approaching three in the morning. Joey must have left Uncle George's cabin sometime after five o'clock. Whenever he'd left, he'd been unaccounted for for at least ten hours now!

Trooper Arbetchian came around the corner of the big house.

"The fingerprint crew are still up at the murder site," he reported to Purdy. "They'll be here in a few minutes. Nothing up there, nothing to work on really."

"Guard this cottage and don't let anyone but the crew in," Purdy ordered. "I'll be in the house when there's anything to report. Can we go in the house, now, Mr. Hopkins?"

Hopkins's hostility seemed to have faded. He hadn't, Uncle George thought, had this much feeling about his own daughter's death. Most of his enormous vitality seemed to have evaporated. He led the way into the big house and across the entrance hall into his study. Someone had built a wood fire in the fireplace and Uncle George found himself instinctively reaching out his hands to the flame. He was chilled, either from the cold fall morning, or by his anxiety for Joey. Hopkins moved around behind his flat-topped desk and sat down. For a moment he lifted his hands and pressed his fingertips against his eyelids.

"How much can you be expected to take in twenty-four hours?" he asked no one in particular.

"About Bradshaw," Purdy said. He had taken a notebook and a ballpoint pen out of the tunic of his uniform.

Hopkins took a deep breath and lowered his hands. "His legal name is—was—Joel Bradshaw, Junior. He was called Joe to distinguish him from his father, who was always Joel."

"We need to notify his family," Purdy said.

"There's no one to notify," Hopkins said. "His mother died more than ten years ago. Joel Bradshaw, Senior, only outlived her by a couple of years."

"Brothers, sisters, a wife?" Purdy asked.

Hopkins shook his head. The firelight flickered on his face that was so startlingly like the late Clark Gable's. "Only child," he said. "Not married."

"How old was he?" Purdy asked.

"Thirty-five or -six. I think his last birthday was his thirty-sixth. We gave a little party for him here at Hilltop."

"I take it he wasn't just a hired watchman to you?"

"Because I gave him a party?" Hopkins's smile was wry.

125

"But you're right, Captain. Joe's father, Joel, Senior, was a longtime friend and business associate of mine. Young Joe grew up at his family's place out on Long Island—Oyster Bay. Went to school, college—Princeton. Good athlete. Played football and hockey. Honor student. Then the Air Force and the war in Vietnam. He was in Intelligence there. He came back when it was over, needed a job like most of those young men. My corporate interests involve a pretty complex kind of climate—industrial technology needed by emerging countries, mostly in the Middle East. We deal with some pretty weird characters in that Arab world. You don't know who you can trust and who's ready to slip a knife in your ribs. So we have a pretty complex security system. Joe, Junior, was trained for it and I was glad to be able to fit him into my picture. He was first rate at the job."

"Then you brought him here as a bodyguard for you?"

Hopkins laughed. "I don't need a bodyguard, Captain. I can take care of myself. Joe's mother died and then, I think three years later, his father died. He wasn't left as well off as he'd had a right to expect. His father had made some pretty unwise investments. But young Joe was doing very well with the Hopkins Corporation."

"'Very well' meaning what?" Purdy asked.

"Forty-five, fifty thousand a year," Hopkins said. "His was a high-risk job and he was well paid for it."

"And winds up being a nursemaid to an attack dog?" Purdy asked.

A muscle rippled along Hopkins's jaw. "Be good enough to let me give you the information you want, Captain, and don't ask me to play Ping-Pong with your guesses." He waited for Purdy to say something but Purdy just gave him that cold-eyed trooper look. Hopkins went on. "A couple of years ago young Bradshaw was on an assignment for the Hopkins corporation in Lebanon. Crazy place—Jews, Syrians, Lebanese, the PLO all shooting at each other. Some-

126

body threw a grenade into the car in which Joe, Junior, was riding; killed the driver and the front-seat passenger, and Joe and another man were carted off to the hospital, badly wounded. Shrapnel from the grenade ripped up Joe pretty badly in his gut. He was shipped back to this country after a couple of months. No place to go to recuperate. I insisted he come up here. Delia, my wife, was happy to have him.

"His recuperation was slow. You can ask Dr. Walters. Joe finally insisted he couldn't go on being a guest in the house forever. We'd had a couple of minor break-ins here. You know; they were reported to you. I suggested to Joe that he move into the cottage and take on the job of a kind of private security force for his place. It wasn't a matter of his taking a low salary. He's on leave from the corporation, disabled, drawing his regular salary. Anyway, Joe bought the idea. Job would keep him outdoors in the country, which he loved. Also he'd have privacy. He decided to train an attack dog and he did. How much longer he would have stayed here—" Hopkins shrugged. "Dr. Walters will tell you he'd have been very soon fit enough to go back to his regular job."

"You think this could be related to his regular job?" Purdy asked. "Someone in your business world out to get him?"

"He never hinted to me that he was in danger from anyone." Hopkins hesitated. "The whole damned world is filled with crazy people."

"Was young Paul Comargo ever connected with your corporation in any way Hopkins?" Uncle George asked.

"Hell, no! He was a boy Anne met in college. A no-good lecher! I told you, I found him squirming around in Anne's bed here at Hilltop and I kicked him out, warned him to stay away from Anne."

"Bradshaw knew this?"

"Sure. I told him what had happened. I told him if Comargo ever came snooping around here again he should throw him out on his butt."

"And then you got him kicked out of college, hounded him out of several jobs," Uncle George said.

"No! I've already told you I had nothing to do with any of that. I *did* let the dean at the college know what had happened here, but I don't know why he was expelled and I certainly don't know anything about the jobs he lost."

"We're wasting time with Comargo, George," Purdy said. "Bradshaw was alive and well long after Comargo was dead. You saw him here at the front gate yourself when you were first looking for Joey."

"Comargo told Anne, according to her, that he was coming here to tell Hopkins something that would get him off his back."

"So?" Purdy asked.

"A far-out suggestion," Uncle George said, "but Hopkins ordered Bradshaw to throw Comargo out on his butt if he showed up at Hilltop. Did he choose to do it by burying him alive up on my place?"

"Oh, for God's sake!" Hopkins exploded.

"And leave a warning message in Marilyn Stroud's mailbox?" Purdy asked.

"At that time he was 'alive and well and living in Paris,' to coin a cliché," Uncle George said. "He was alive and well in the middle of the day, yesterday, when someone put a warning in Marilyn Stroud's mailbox. He was alive and well when Joey set out to look for evidence."

"And then he beat himself to death up there on the hill?" Hopkins said, his anger rising again. "Wouldn't it make sense, Captain Purdy, to keep this daydreaming creep out of this investigation? He's been alive, and well, and circulating where he shouldn't while all this was happening."

A trooper came in from the entrance hall. Uncle George knew his name was Fred Sumner.

"We've been over this house, Captain, top to bottom," he said. "No sign of Joey Trimble or that he's ever been here in the house. Nothing else that seems to mean anything."

Uncle George felt, suddenly, bone tired. "I think I'll head back over the hill to my place," he said, "so I can pick up my Jeep. I need to circulate down below where Red Egan and his people are still looking for the boy."

"You're not going to let him go, are you, Captain?" Hopkins asked.

"I'll know where to find him when I need him," Purdy said.

The early mornings at that time of the year are apt to be quite cold in New England, low teens, Uncle George guessed. His own feeling of chill wasn't due, however, to the position of the thermometer. He kept thinking of what must be Joey's state of mind—if Joey was alive to have feelings. If he was hurt and unable to call for help it must be agony for the boy to be aware that half the town was looking for him and that he couldn't somehow signal for help. If he was being held prisoner he must know that his jailers were responsible for what had happened to Paul Comargo, for what had happened to Anne Hopkins. Joey might well have discovered what *had* happened to Anne, which was why he was being held. To be used as some kind of pawn or bargaining chip if the law began to get too close? Joey was far too bright not to guess at such a possibility and he must be living in terror.

Uncle George shut his mind to the possibility that Joey wasn't feeling anything at all, had been silenced in the same brutal fashion as Bradshaw.

Two troopers with electric lanterns shining brightly were

129

at the spot where Bradshaw had died when Uncle George climbed the hill toward the ridge that would take him across the hillside to his own property. One of them stepped forward, shining his light on Uncle George.

"Crowder? You going somewhere?" It was a trooper named Pat Doyle.

"Home," Uncle George said.

"I can't let you go without an okay from the captain," Doyle said.

"He gave me permission to leave, Pat."

"I'll have to check," Doyle said. He had some kind of walkie-talkie radio hanging by a leather strap around his neck. He switched it on and spoke into it. "Doyle calling Captain Purdy, Doyle calling Captain Purdy." He switched it over to "receive" and waited. After a few moments Purdy's voice came to them.

"Purdy here. What is it, Pat?"

"Okay to let George Crowder leave the property?"

"You can let him go."

"Did the fingerprint boys get to you?"

"They're in the cottage now, but I haven't talked to them."

"We think we found the weapon, Captain," Doyle said. "Iron wrecking bar, like Doc Walters suggested. Covered with blood, pieces of stuff that could be hair, skin, maybe even brains."

"God Almighty, handle it carefully. Where was it?"

"Thirty-five or forty yards from where Bradshaw was attacked. Could have been thrown there when the killer was through with it. Don't worry, Sergeant Terry's on his way to the lab with it. He'll report to you as soon as he knows anything. I was just about to come down to the house to tell you about it."

"So maybe we've got something at last," Purdy said. "Let Crowder go. Sit tight."

The radio was switched off.

"A wrecking bar?" Uncle George asked.

"Iron bar, sort of a sharp-pointed hook on one end and a chisel-shaped tip on the other. Used for opening crates and boxes. What do you make of all this, George?"

"Someone so viciously crazy it's hard to imagine," Uncle George said, his voice harsh. "No sign that Joey was around here anywhere?"

"Nothing," Doyle said. "We aren't supposed to move very far from this spot. Special detectives are on their way from the state headquarters. We have to keep things untouched till they get here."

"More chiefs than Indians," Uncle George said. "I'll be on my way."

"Good luck, George. The boy's bound to show up."

"If we find him," Uncle George said. "He'd be here now if he could show up on his own."

The mile walk across the ridge to his own side of the hill was cold and dreary. He kept shining his torch to one side and then the other on the path. If Joey had been on the Hopkins property and tried to go for help he might have come this way. There was no place to fall—no cliff, or well, or pond. An accident, beyond a sprained ankle, wasn't in the cards on this stretch of country. The encounter between Timmy, the setter, and Charlie, the attack boxer, must have taken place inside the Hopkins boundaries—unless Bradshaw had been away from the property with his dog. Joey had to be somewhere back there on the Hilltop grounds.

Uncle George stopped, almost turned back, and then managed to convince himself that Purdy's troopers would, sooner or later, cover every possible hiding place at Hilltop, lift every stone, turn back every blade of grass. Daylight would eventually come—it always had. In daylight the chance to find some positive clues as to what had happened to Joey would radically increase. Only a very few hours and Uncle George knew he would have to redouble his energies. He needed that much rest. He was dead on his feet.

He walked slowly down the hill at the other end of the ridge, past that grim hole in the earth where Paul Comargo had been buried, and toward the dark shape of his un-lighted cabin. It was an odd feeling to arrive home without his trusted friend, Timmy the setter, there to greet him.

He reached into his pocket for his keys as he walked up the front steps. He focused his flash on the front door lock and was instantly aware of something unusual, a piece of white paper that seemed to be Scotch-taped to the door. He turned his light on it and felt his mouth go dry.

On the paper, possibly an ordinary piece of typewriter paper, was a drawing. It was of something like a rectangular box. From the top of the drawn box there was a little picture of what could be a piece of string—or something resembling a piece of plastic tubing!

Under the drawing, in precise capital letters, was a message.

YOU ARE HEADED FOR THIS IF YOU DON'T
KNOCK IT OFF

Uncle George hesitated a moment, and then, without touching the paper, he unlocked the cabin door and went in, switching on the lights. He stood by the door, which opened inward, looking at the drawing again in bright in-side light. He had left here at about eight o'clock that night after returning from the barracks where he'd taken Marilyn Stroud. He'd found Joey and the dog missing, guessed where they had gone, and set out to find them. This crude message had been stuck to his door after that! The same person who had left a message for Marilyn Stroud in the early afternoon had visited him that evening—knowing that he wasn't at the cabin.

He went over to the kitchen table and took a sharp-pointed little paring knife from the drawer. Then he tore off a piece of paper toweling from the rack on the pantry wall. Back at the front door, he took hold of the bottom of the drawing with the piece of paper towel. With the little knife he pried loose the Scotch tape that held it in place. He carried the drawing in, without ever touching it with his fingers, put it down on the center table, covered it with the piece of toweling, and put the table saltshaker on it to hold it in place. He went back, closed the front door, and locked it.

There was a pot of cold coffee on the stove. Thank God he'd installed electricity and his own generator a while back. He put the coffee over a burner and turned it on high. A few moments later he poured himself a steaming mug of hot black coffee and took it over to the table. He sat down, still huddled in Red Egan's parka, and stared at the paper towel that covered the warning drawing.

Knock off what? The State Police, the sheriff and his deputies, and the presently-to-arrive State Police detectives were concentrating on the murders of Joel Bradshaw and Paul Comargo. Uncle George's participation in those investigations could add very little to the killer's danger. But he was the one person who had stubbornly refused to accept the fact that Anne Hopkins's death had been an accident. He had suggested that to Red Egan, and Captain Purdy, and perhaps, more importantly, to Delia Hopkins. Marilyn Stroud had been warned, and she had no connection with anyone involved in all this violence but Anne. Joey had only been interested in finding some clue to what had really happened to Anne. Timmy, the setter, had been attacked and hurt when he was trying to follow a trail suggested to him by the nightgown Uncle George had taken from Anne's clothes closet at Hilltop. Add all these facts together and they spelled just two words—Anne Hopkins. That's what Uncle George was supposed to "knock off." He was being warned to forget about Anne. If he didn't he'd get the same treatment Paul Comargo had. Or was he meant to guess that Joey would be the victim if his uncle persisted in searching for the truth about the girl?

The coffee helped, but not much. He got up and went to the corner cupboard. He brought a bottle of bourbon whiskey from it and laced the coffee with a couple of ounces. He began to feel warmer as he sipped.

He could back off, wipe his hands of the whole thing, and pray for Joey's safety. He could make it publicly clear that he was no longer involving himself in the case. He could leave town, go away somewhere, to let them know he'd "knocked it off." But if Joey was a prisoner would they ever be able to let him go? He would be able to identify someone.

There was no way he could knock it off. There was only the chance that if he moved quickly, quietly, and successfully he might save the boy before the killer lost patience, or saw that Joey was no longer someone he could use to barter.

Deep in his heart Uncle George knew that if he failed, whatever was left on his own life would be spent in searching for a killer and becoming one himself.

But where to start again?

Long ago Uncle George had taught himself how to get rest when his work load required long, consecutive hours of attention. He could relax, tell himself that he had an hour or two to sleep, and wake up exactly the moment he'd set for himself, as if he had an internal alarm clock. It would be about two hours and a half till daylight, he knew, and daylight was almost essential in which to continue the search for Joey or for some clue as to what had happened to him.

He didn't undress, as would have been his usual custom. With someone running around sticking signs on doors and into mailboxes, he wanted to be able to move instantly if he had to. His handgun was still in the possession of the troopers up at Hilltop, and so he got himself a rifle out of the gun rack on the far wall, put it down beside him on the bed, covered himself with a patchwork quilt Esther had made for him, closed his eyes, and waited for sleep to overtake him.

Not this time.

His mind insisted on going back to the piece of plastic tubing Marilyn Stroud had found in her mailbox, with the note wrapped around it, the note that warned her she had already stuck her neck out too far, that threatened her with a living burial.

Sticking out her neck had been Marilyn's giving Uncle George a lead to the identity of Paul Comargo, and revealing Anne Hopkins's secret way of communicating with her lover. What could Marilyn do, beyond that, which would be dangerous to the killer? Was there something she still hadn't told him? Something she felt was Anne's secret and that her dead friend wouldn't have wanted revealed? Part of the girl's love relationship with Comargo? How could that kind of secret lead to the killer?

Hours ago Lucius Hopkins had been at the top of Uncle George's list of potential killers. Hopkins was, in fact, the only name on that list because no other names had emerged. He had, according to Marilyn, thrown Comargo out of his house, had him expelled from college, continued his persecution by costing Comargo job after job. That was still hearsay, until Lieutenant Kreevich had checked out in the city and confirmed it. In a few hours they might have that answer. But Lucius Hopkins would surely not have risked fooling around Marilyn's mailbox in broad daylight. Everyone in Lakeview knew him by sight. If a stranger, say, some "leaf-peeper" passing through town, saw him his description would have left no doubt: "A man who looks just like the late Clark Gable with gray hair."

Lucius Hopkins had been in bed with his wife the night before when the tragedy at the swimming pool, whatever it had been, had taken place. He couldn't have been physically involved—unless his wife was lying for him. The notion that Delia Hopkins was lying to shield her husband in the murder of her beloved daughter simply could not be bought. Hopkins had the power, the money, the influence to buy a hit-man. To kill his stepdaughter? To kill his friend and employee, Joel Bradshaw? To scatter threats around the community? Possible, but somehow, hard to swallow. Hopkins would have placed himself in a position to be blackmailed for the rest of his life.

That brought the sleepless Uncle George to Bradshaw, a protégé and friend of Hopkins. Had Comargo known something about Bradshaw he planned to reveal to Hopkins and been killed before he could act? Why the elaborate burial alive? That had to be a message to someone, Uncle George thought, just as it had now been a message to Marilyn and to him. Had Anne Hopkins known that secret from Comargo and planned to reveal it to her mother and stepfather before she went to the police? Bradshaw could have waylaid her when she got home and faked the suicide in the pool. But then, who had killed Bradshaw? It was far more likely that Bradshaw was innocent of any crime, but had discovered who was, been intercepted, and beaten to death.

The music goes round and round, Uncle George thought. Sleep did not come.

The killer had to have access to the Hilltop grounds, he thought. True, the killer could have come to Hilltop the

136

way he had. But if he was right about Anne, Uncle George knew that the killer had to be someone close to the setup there; someone who could have moved around the house freely, taken clothes from Anne's closet to replace the ones she'd been wearing when she died—the pink shirt, the blue slacks, the blue quilted jacket. That brought him to Jerry Hopkins, his two friends, Girard and Lawrence, the staff of servants only one of whom Uncle George had so far met—the Clarkson girl. Not likely the little blond maid could have beaten Bradshaw to death with an iron bar, or thrown Anne into an empty swimming pool, or buried Comargo alive.

So, what about the three young men? If one of them had killed Bradshaw, the others had to know. They'd all been searching the grounds for Joey. If that was the case, they were all in it together. They could alibi each other forever. But motive? If there was one, it was hidden deep for the moment.

Uncle George's eyelids had grown heavy and they closed, only to pop open again. He had forgotten one person on the inside at Hilltop. Martin, the mechanic and sometimes pilot for Lucius Hopkins's fleet of cars and his plane; Martin who had come to the gates the first time Uncle George had gone there to ask questions.

Round and round again. There were all these people from the outside, about whom he knew nothing, who were also on the inside. There was no way to guess at motives for people like Girard and Lawrence and Martin. There was really no way to guess at motives for anyone. The whole Hopkins crew lived here, and yet they were strangers. Marilyn Stroud might know more, learned from Anne, if she could be persuaded to talk.

Uncle George opened his eyes, and it was daylight! He'd slept after all, and waked himself at exactly the time he'd set for himself—seven o'clock. He lay still for a moment, trying to reorganize the thoughts he'd had before he'd blacked out. Then he heard a sound, someone coughing outside the cabin.

No one came to the door, no one knocked or called out. But the cough was repeated. Quietly, Uncle George threw back the quilt that had kept him warm, picked up his rifle, and threw his feet over the side of the bed. He stood up and walked to the window next to the porch. Sitting on the front step, smoking a cigarette, was a man he'd never seen before. This was a young man, dark-bearded, wearing what could only be described as city clothes—a black raglan overcoat, a blue scarf at his neck, a gray tweed hat set rather jauntily on his dark hair, which was worn long down the back of his neck.

Rifle at the ready, Uncle George opened the cabin door and stepped out onto the porch.

"You want something here?" he asked.

The young man turned his head and then stood up. He had bright blue eyes and a smile that was meant to charm.

"Mr. Crowder? I knew you must be resting and I didn't want to disturb you, but I didn't want to miss you when you got ready to leave. Like most of the people in this town I knew you must have been on the go, round the clock. I'm Norman Perkins of the International Press."

A reporter!

"What can I do for you?" Uncle George asked.

"Talk, if you will."

"I don't know that I will, Mr. Perkins, but come in out of the cold. Looks like a good day coming up, but cold."

Perkins followed his host into the cabin.

"Nice place," he said. "Every kid's dream of the kind of place to retire to."

"Look, Perkins, if you are covering this Lakeview horror story you will know that my twelve-year-old nephew is missing, has been for more than twelve hours. My only concern at the moment is to find him. I don't have time for an interview. I'm going to reheat some old coffee, shave, put on a clean shirt, and take off. If you have something you want to ask while I'm doing those things, start asking." He turned to the stove and turned on the heat under last-night's coffee. He glanced at Perkins. "You want to sit on the john cover while I shave, you're welcome."

"It's my pleasure," Perkins said. "It's the boy I wanted to ask about." He followed Uncle George into the bathroom, put down the top of the john seat, and perched there.

"What's to ask?" Uncle George said. He washed his face, and then lathered it with some kind of foaming gel.

"It's all over town, Mr. Crowder, that the boy set out to do a job that you had planned to do yourself—backtrack on Anne Hopkins. You had to help a friend who was in some kind of trouble, and the boy decided to take over for you."

"If that's what the whole town is saying, who am I to question them?" Uncle George asked.

"Why backtrack on Anne Hopkins, I asked myself," Perkins said. "Mind if I smoke a cigarette?"

"No—but it won't do that cough of yours any good."

Perkins took a cigarette out of his pocket, slipped a lighter into flame, inhaled, coughed. He smiled at Uncle George. "You could be right about the cough. But why backtrack on Anne Hopkins, I keep asking myself. In this little town that's gone murder crazy in the last thirty-six hours, the unfortunate accident that resulted in the girl's death doesn't seem to fit. I've found out a little bit about you, Mr. Crowder, since I hit town. If you think there's something odd about Anne Hopkins's death, then maybe there is."

Uncle George looked at his own lathered face in the mirror. Let this reporter spread the word and it would be everywhere, newspapers, radio, television. The person who'd left that warning note on his door would be certain he hadn't "knocked it off." He began shaving, not looking at Perkins.

"If you've been working on this story, Mr. Perkins, you know that Paul Comargo, the man who was buried alive just up the lane here, was a beau of Anne Hopkins. She went to the hospital morgue with Sheriff Egan and me and saw that her young man was dead. She was naturally in shock. She left us about two o'clock and headed for home, only a little over a mile away. She didn't get there until four o'clock, according to Bradshaw, the night watchman. Anne had asked me for help. I was concerned with what had happened, where she had been for that two hours."

"I understand she'd asked you to be her lawyer," Perkins said. "Why did she need a lawyer?"

Uncle George looked at himself steadily in the mirror. The right side of his face was shaved. "To represent Comargo's interests. He apparently had no family or anyone to act for him."

"She identified Comargo in the hospital morgue, you say, and yet you sent to New York for someone to identify him all over again," Perkins said.

Uncle George bent down and washed the remnants of soap off his face. Then he took a hand towel from the rack and dried his face. He turned to the reporter. "You have been doing your homework, Mr. Perkins. Anne was no longer alive to repeat that identification to the police. We had to have someone who could make that identification official." He walked past Perkins and out into the main room. From the bureau he got himself a clean shirt and put it on. Perkins had followed him.

"You have some theories about what Anne did in the two hours she took to drive a mile?" he asked.

"Several simple possibilities," Uncle George said, buttoning his shirt. "As I told you, she was in shock. She could have driven a short way, pulled her car over to the side of the road, and sat there, trying to pull herself together. She could have had a flat tire, waited for someone to come along to help her. When no one came, she might have changed it herself. That could all have taken a lot of time in her state of mind. She could have visited a friend who hasn't come forward yet to tell us. In any case, I wanted to know. It was something missing in the picture."

"Why would a friend hold back?"

"For no reason I can think of, which is why I don't think that's what happened."

"How did the boy, your nephew, get involved in this?"

"He came here to visit me. I had to go see a friend who was in trouble. I told him what I planned to do—about Anne—when I'd taken care of my friend."

"And he took your dog and went to do the job himself?"

Uncle George took another topcoat of his from the closet. He was ready to go. "We've played games— detective games—quite often, the boy and I. I guess he hoped to surprise me with something he might find."

"And the dog got chewed up, but no boy. What do you think has happened to him, Mr. Crowder?"

*You are headed for this if you don't knock it off.* "Who knows?" Uncle George said. "He heard Timmy, the dog, fighting with some other animal, ran to help him, fell, knocked himself out."

"That was hours and hours ago," Perkins said. "Wouldn't you have found him near the dog?"

"The dog could have dragged himself a long way from the scene of his fight. We've just got to keep looking. Now, if you'll excuse me, Perkins, that's what I've got to get to. Looking."

"Thanks. My car's down at the main road. Can I come back again if something turns up?"

"Joey is all I want to have turn up." Uncle George got a large manila envelope out of the drawer of his desk. Using

141

another piece of paper towel he managed to slip the message that had been stuck to his door into the envelope, without touching it directly. Perkins watched this rather awkward process without asking any question about it. "Hang on, I'll drive you down to your car."

Perkins asked his last question on the way down the logging road in Uncle George's Jeep to his parked car. "You think someone local has gone berserk, Mr. Crowder? It couldn't be someone from the outside who just happened to choose this area for a senseless violence?"

Uncle George gave the reporter a quick glance and then focused back on the rough trail. "You're not serious, are you, Perkins?"

"Oh, I know Anne Hopkins and Comargo were lovers. I know Bradshaw was Lucius Hopkins's protégé, friend, and employee. The whole madness seems to be aimed at the Hopkinses. But could it be some crazy radical, incensed by all the signs of wealth—big house, private plane, a half-dozen expensive cars, locked gates, and attack dog?"

Uncle George stopped the Jeep beside a parked car at the side of the main highway. "There's something that always happens when there's a butchering of this sort, Perkins. People invent the damnedest explanations for it. They almost never have anything to do with the facts in the case."

Perkins gave Uncle George his bright smile. "What's your invention, Mr. Crowder?"

Uncle George leaned back behind the wheel, fingering the manila envelope he'd brought with him. "Burying Comargo alive with that plastic tube sticking out of his coffin wasn't original. You must remember a case like it about a year ago in Texas. The killer wasn't trying to conceal a crime. He wanted it discovered and to get all the publicity it has gotten. My invention, Perkins, is that he meant to get a message to someone. 'Stop whatever it is you're doing, or this will come your way, too.' I can imagine a group of men together, perhaps involved in some kind of criminal conspiracy. They read about that case in Texas. I can imagine one of them saying: 'What a way to torture and punish a man! If anyone ever betrays us I think I'll know how to make him regret it.'"

"And you think Comargo was one of those men?"

"Pure invention, Perkins, not based on a single fact. Some of my friends think I ought to be writing for television."

"And Bradshaw?"

Uncle George shrugged. "Could be pure coincidence," he said. "His job was to keep trespassers off the Hilltop property. Hilltop has invited trespassers since the word got out that there was a connection there with Comargo. Bradshaw tried to take the trespasser in and wasn't up to the job."

"Also invention?"

"That's what you asked for, wasn't it, Perkins? Now, if you'll excuse me, I've got to get a move on."

Purdy wasn't at the barracks. According to the trooper on the desk he'd gone home to try to get a few minutes of rest.

"Been on the go, right round the clock," the trooper said. "Unless it's an emergency—"

"I brought this," Uncle George said, putting his brown envelope down on the desk. "A warning pasted to my front door. I made sure I didn't touch it with my bare hands. The lab may be able to pick up some fingerprints. If they match anything they found on the coffin, or in Bradshaw's cottage, or on the weapon that killed Bradshaw, or in the main house, we may be getting somewhere. Marilyn Stroud still here?"

The trooper nodded. "She's free to come and go, but I

143

think she's still in the cell down that corridor, third one on the right. I saw her at the coffee machine, a little while back."

Marilyn was sitting, rather rigidly, on the edge of the cot in the cell she'd been provided with for a night's lodging. She looked relieved at the sight of Uncle George.

"Boy, am I glad to see you, George!"

"Get some rest?" he asked.

"This is not exactly the Waldorf-Astoria," she said. "Iron doors banging, men shouting to each other, two driving-while-intoxicateds for my neighbors! I heard about Joey, George. Have you found him?"

Uncle George shook his head. "I hoped maybe you could help."

"I? How could I help?"

Uncle George sat down on the edge of the cot beside Marilyn. "I'm a bad influence on that boy, you know," he said. "Filling his mind with trashy nonsense, teaching him useless skills."

"Oh, come on, George. That's Hector Trimble speaking!"

"But he's right, you know," Uncle George said. "His smile was grim. "Joey's missing because of what I've put into his head, and because of those useless skills I taught him."

"You'll have to try me again on that one," Marilyn said.

"Sherlock Holmes," Uncle George said. "I read him most of the Conan Doyle stories about Holmes and Dr. Watson. We often played games. I was Holmes and he was Watson."

"So what's wrong with that?"

"Yesterday afternoon, when I got back to my place after being at Hilltop to talk to the Hopkinses, I found Joey there. I told you I was looking for the clothes Anne was wearing when I'd last seen her and which weren't the things found in the bathhouse?"

Marilyn nodded.

"I'd snitched a nightgown of Anne's from her closet. I thought I could take my dog, Timmy, back to the hospital and that the nightgown might put him on the trail of where Anne had gone after she left Red and me the night before. Joey had a message from you that you needed help. It told him what I was planning to do about Anne when I got back from you. When I did get back, after leaving you here, Joey was gone, also the dog, also the nightgown, and a rifle from my gun rack. He could have written me a note. He'd gone to see if he could help me by finding a clue to Anne. Watson taking over for Holmes. The trash I'd put in his head. He wasn't afraid, even though everyone knew there was some kind of murderous psycho loose in town. He wasn't afraid, because of the useless skills I'd taught him. He can shoot a specific crabapple out of a tree with a rifle. Without the trash and the special useless skills, he'd have gone home to supper, done his homework, and gone to bed! So, you see, I'm to blame."

"Nonsense," Marilyn said. "But how am I supposed to be able to help?"

"By not having any secrets from me, Marilyn."

"I don't understand. What secrets?"

"Anne told you that Comargo was coming here last week because he thought he had something that would get Lucius Hopkins 'off his back.' Right?"

"Yes."

"What? What would get Hopkins off his back?"

"I don't know, George."

"Something that would make Hopkins grateful to him? Something with which he could threaten Hopkins?"

"I don't know. All she said was, something that would get her father off Paul's back."

"You can't help Anne by clamming up now, Marilyn. The person who killed her—and I'm sure she was killed—is threatening you, is threatening me."

"You, George?"

"Picture of a coffin with a piece of tubing sticking out of it Scotch-taped to my front door during the night. I'm to 'knock it off.' So you see it isn't safe to hold back anything you think might protect Anne, or Paul Comargo, or even Anne's mother."

"I swear to you, George, I've told you everything I know."

He sighed. "Well, if you haven't, it could be, as the man says, 'your funeral.'"

"George!"

"You can't anticipate a lunatic," Uncle George said. "Another approach to this, Marilyn. Anne was close to you. She must have talked to you about many things that were critical to her—like her affair with Comargo. Pleasant memories, unhappy memories. I wondered if she ever mentioned some special place she liked to go."

"I don't think I understand."

"'When I was a kid there was a special place I liked to go—to think, to play a certain game.' What I'm getting at is that, in the terrible shock she must have felt at seeing Comargo in the hospital morgue, she might have gone to that special place that has represented some kind of security to her."

"She never mentioned any such place to me," Marilyn said. "Remember, George, Anne didn't spend her childhood at Hilltop. The Hopkinses only bought the place five or six years ago. She was away from here much of the time, private school and college."

Uncle George stood up. "Well, it was worth a try," he said.

"What am I supposed to do now, George? I can't settle in here forever. I had wondered whether your sister would take me in for a few days, but now she has her own troubles."

"I'll talk to Red Egan when I catch up with him," Uncle George said. "He'll set something up for you. I've got to get back to the searching. Hold the fort."

"One thing, George!" she called out to him as he stepped out into the corridor. "There must be some maps of the old Crane place—Hilltop—before the Hopkinses bought it. Could be in the town hall, or perhaps the local real estate offices. There could be some old abandoned well, or something, into which Joey could have fallen."

"Bless you! It's worth a try," Uncle George said.

The desk sergeant was coming down the hall.

"Stan Boswell, the State Police homicide detective, just got here," he said. "I showed him the warning you found stuck to your door. He wants to talk to you. He's in the captain's office."

# 4

Boswell was a big blond man with restless brown eyes.

"Glad I found you here, Crowder," he said. "The desk man just showed me what you brought in. A schoolteacher got a warning, too, I understand."

"Yes, Marilyn Stroud. I brought her here last night. It didn't seem safe to leave her alone."

"What is it you're supposed to 'knock off,' Crowder?"

Uncle George hesitated.

"I haven't had a chance to talk to Purdy yet," Boswell said. "He's on his way. But I know a little something about you, Crowder. I know you're not someone caught up in some kind of hysteria. I know about your lost nephew, but I'm not clear about how it happened."

Uncle George made a judgment about Boswell. The man was a solid professional. That kind of help was what they

147

needed. Boswell wearing civilian clothes, he couldn't guess what his rank was.

"You a sergeant, lieutenant?" he asked.

"I'm just a cop—special officer," Boswell said. "I know you found this Comargo. Buried alive on your property, wasn't he? What does that message mean—'knock it off'? You know something you haven't told Purdy? You playing some lead all by yourself?"

"So much has happened around here in the last hours, Boswell. Comargo, the accidental death of Anne Hopkins, the murder of Bradshaw, the watchman at Hilltop. There are so many different places to start. Purdy and the sheriff began with Comargo. That's where they're still at. I had a different starting point. That's what I'm supposed to 'knock off,' I think."

"Time's wasting, Crowder. Let me have it."

"Purdy didn't buy it when I told him, but here it is." Uncle George drew a deep breath. "The first thing, after we found Comargo, was to identify him." He told the detective how Anne Hopkins had been covering the case for the local newspaper, how she had asked to see the body. She'd thought it might be her boyfriend, told them of family difficulties there were about him. He and Red Egan had taken her to the morgue to look, and she'd said it wasn't anyone she knew.

"Neither Red nor I believed her," Uncle George said.

They'd watched her drive off for home. The next thing they knew about her was that she'd decided to take a swim in the early hours of a cold morning, dived, naked, into an empty pool and brained herself.

"Purdy and the family wrote it off as a tragic accident, but somehow I couldn't swallow it."

He told the rest of it, the wrong clothes in the bathhouse, the cooperation offered by Delia Hopkins, the failure to find the clothes Anne had been wearing earlier.

He'd told how his sister had put him onto Marilyn Stroud. It was a bull's-eye. Identification followed with the help of Lieutenant Kreevich and Lewis, Comargo's friend in New York. He told about the stolen nightgown and what he planned doing with it; how Joey had come with a message that Marilyn Stroud needed him.

"I told the boy what I was planning, and I went off to Marilyn's place. She'd found her warning in the mailbox and was scared out of her wits. I brought her here, and Purdy put her up in a cell for the night. He didn't have anyone he could spare to watch-dog her. When I got back to my cabin my nephew was gone, also my setter, the nightgown, and a rifle. It was clear what Joey had set out to do, give me a hand. Somewhere, along the way, he must have wandered onto the Hopkins property. Timmy, the setter, got into a fight with the attack dog there. We found him, some distance away from Hilltop, badly chewed up. But no sign of the boy, not then, not later, not after a careful search of all the buildings and the grounds at Hilltop. In that time the night watchman, Bradshaw, was beaten to death."

"You have a theory about that?" Boswell asked.

Uncle George shrugged. "He could have encountered a trespasser who was too much for him."

"You sound as though you didn't believe that either," Boswell said.

"You know that we searched his cottage? It had been ripped apart, one of his dogs there with his throat cut. The whole thing smells, Boswell, but I haven't got a handle on it. The one thing I hadn't been too quiet about was that I suspected Anne Hopkins, too, had been murdered. That's what I'm supposed to 'knock off,' I think. I will get the full treatment if I don't—or Joey will."

Boswell was doodling on a pad on Purdy's desk. "If it's any comfort to you, Crowder, I'm inclined to go along with

149

you about the Hopkins girl. She goes home at two o'clock in the morning, after seeing her boyfriend on a morgue slab. She changes her clothes, apparently planning to go out again, then changes her mind, undresses, and dives into an empty pool. I suppose a girl in shock might behave that erratically, but I don't like it."

"Bradshaw, the watchman, told us that he heard her come home about four o'clock," Uncle George said. "That leaves close to two hours unaccounted for."

"If Bradshaw was telling the truth. No way now to pressure him about that," Boswell said.

"I've wondered if he was presenting an alibi for someone," Uncle George said. "She should have been home a few minutes after two. Whoever it was who arrived at four had a key to the gates. All members of the family have keys, some of the servants."

"You're suggesting that Anne's murderer was on the inside. He needed an alibi for the real time she was killed, and Bradshaw gave it to him by saying that Anne came home at four?"

"Could be. Could be she was killed before she ever got home. Her body brought home by someone at four."

"Someone who had a key to the gates."

"Anne had a key. No problem for the killer if he didn't have one of his own."

Boswell tossed his doodling pencil down on the desk. "We have a long way to go, Crowder."

Right now the only thing that concerns me is Joey," Uncle George said. "You've got three separate murder cases, maybe related, maybe not. I wish you luck, friend. Find my boy and it may ease the load on you. Joey has answers—if he can give them to us."

One thing had to be said for the town of Lakeview. The scene of two brutal and bizarre murders, they were in the national spotlight. (The death of Anne Hopkins was still being considered by most people to be a tragic accident.) There were professional people to deal with the murders— the local sheriff, the local State Police, and special officers from the state headquarters of the State Police. There were fingerprint experts, lab technicians, and special techniques available to them. But a missing boy was something else again. Young Joey Trimble was one of them. Over a hundred men who had grown up in the area, knew the woods and the surrounding countryside, had been searching now for long hours without success. George Crowder, his sister, Esther, and her comic-villain of a husband, Hector, were liked, respected, and very much a part of their daily lives. Help for them was given freely, almost eagerly.

Marilyn Stroud's suggestion about old maps of the Hilltop property seemed worth following up to Uncle George. That property consisted of more than a hundred and fifty acres of land. Not more than fifty acres of it had been cultivated, planted with lawns and flower beds and fenced in. Somewhere in the remaining acres there could be some kind of trap into which Joey could have fallen. An old well was a possibility, some kind of steep drop that Joey had missed in the dark. An old map might provide them with places to look.

Uncle George parked his Jeep across the street from the Town Hall and found he couldn't make the short trip from his car to the town clerk's office without being surrounded by concerned friends and local people who knew him by sight. Any news of Joey? Any clues as to what might have happened to him? Were the police making any progress on the murders? "My Bob is out searching." They seemed to come out of nowhere, wishing Joey well, hopeful of a happy answer. What could he tell them? As long as there wasn't bad news he could only hope very soon they would find a simple answer to the boy's disappearance. He knew,

*151*

grimly, that he himself was beginning to doubt the answer would be bearable.

Cora Knowles, who had been Lakeview's town clerk for two decades, was full of questions, but she didn't have the answer that Uncle George was looking for.

"There were maps of the old property when the Cranes owned it," she told Uncle George, "but the real estate agent, who was from out of town, asked for them when he was trying to sell the place to Lucius Hopkins. They never came back here, George. The agent, whose name I may have here, may still have them, or he may have turned them over to Lucius Hopkins."

"I'd like the agent's name."

Searching in her records, Cora came up empty. "I can't remember his name, George. He's never had any other property deals here in Lakeview. Mr. Hopkins would know, of course. Maybe Roy Miller, the local man knows it."

"I'll try him."

"I have an idea, though, George. You know old Rich Pettybone?"

"God, is he still alive? He must be a hundred!"

"I think he's ninety-six. They had a special do for him at the Methodist church when he turned ninety-five. He lives with his granddaughter—the Bob Parkers. He worked for the Cranes way back when they built the place, or just after. He must know the property from one end to the other. He should be able to tell you what you want to know."

Uncle George turned for the door. "Mrs. Parker was just out there on the street," he said. "She told me her husband was looking for Joey."

Betty Parker was still outside the Town Hall with the people who were waiting for news. Uncle George took her aside and told her what he had come to the Town Hall to find.

"Cora has no maps, but she suggested your grandfather might be able to help."

Betty Parker, a pleasant-looking country woman, probably in her early fifties, looked uncertain. "Grandpa did work for the Cranes, for nearly forty years, I think. One of the first things I remember as a very little girl was going up there to the property with him. He loved it as if it was his own."

"Can I talk to him?"

"He's—he's pretty far gone, Mr. Crowder. The last year or two—"

"He'd know if there is any unusual trouble Joey could have gotten into."

"He might, he might not," Mrs. Parker said. "I don't like to say it, Mr. Crowder, but he's pretty much of a vegetable these days."

"Can I try him?"

"Of course. But don't be too optimistic."

She drove her car toward the north end of town. Uncle George followed in his Jeep. The Parkers had a neat little dairy farm there. A curl of smoke came from the stone chimney at the far end of the house.

"Grandpa just sits there all day in front of the fire," Betty Parker told Uncle George. "He's always cold, summer or winter. He just sits there and remembers, I guess."

"Let's hope he remembers what I need to know," Uncle George said.

Uncle George remembered Rich Pettybone, long ago when he was growing up—a rugged old man with a loud laugh and some glorious profanity that George Crowder had admired and envied when he was Joey's age. He remembered his mother telling him he'd better wear ear plugs if he was going to be around old Mr. Pettybone.

What Uncle George found sitting in an old wooden armchair in front of the fireplace, staring down into the red glow on the hearth, was a wraith of the man from long ago.

It was a skeleton of the once tall, broad-shouldered man who used to win the log-cutting contests with his axe at the county fair. Rich Pettybone had withered to nothing, skin stretched over bones; skin that looked as if it might crack open with any sudden movement. Once bright blue eyes were watery and blurred. The old man's lips trembled over broken and discolored teeth.

Uncle George pulled up a chair and sat down beside him. "I don't know if you remember me, Mr. Pettybone. I'm George Crowder."

The old man nodded, and kept nodding. A little drool of saliva ran out of the corner of his mouth which he made no effort to wipe away.

"You must have heard what's been going on in town. Some pretty bad violence."

The old man continued to nod and nod. It occurred to Uncle George that the nodding didn't mean "yes." Old Rich Pettybone couldn't control the shaky movement of his head.

"You must know my sister, Esther Trimble," Uncle George said. "Her husband runs the drugstore." The old head nodded and nodded. "Her boy, Joey, is lost somewhere up around the old Crane property. Half the town is out looking for him. Betty's husband is among them."

The old man's lips trembled as if he wanted to speak, but no sound came.

"Cora Knowles, the town clerk, told me you know every inch of that property, Mr. Pettybone. There aren't any maps. I thought you might be able to tell me where he might have gotten into trouble."

The nodding seemed to be more vigorous, but no words came from the trembling lips.

"He can't control the way his head shakes up and down," Betty Parker said, from behind Uncle George in the room. "I'm afraid this isn't his day, Mr. Crowder."

154

"If you could tell me anything that would be helpful I'd be grateful to you forever, Mr. Pettybone," Uncle George said.

The old man nodded, a little more energetically, Uncle George thought. His lips writhed over the broken teeth, but no words came. Uncle George stood up.

"Well, thanks for trying," he said. He turned to leave.

"I'm sorry," Betty Parker said, "but you see how it is."

Uncle George started for the door, and a sound came from the old man. He was trying desperately to speak. Uncle George turned back. Old Rich Pettybone had spoken two words. They sounded like "root cellar."

"Did you say 'root cellar,' Mr. Pettybone?"

The nodding was almost eager.

"Where is it, Mr. Pettybone?"

The two words came gurgling up out of the skinny throat. "Root cellar!"

"Where is it, Mr. Pettybone?"

The old man lifted a skin-and-bones arm high above his head and let it fall onto the arm of the chair.

"Somewhere at the top of the property?" Uncle George asked.

The old man's chin had fallen forward on his chest. He was, clearly, totally exhausted by the effort he'd made.

"Someone at Hilltop will know where it is," Uncle George said to Betty Parker. "When he comes around try to let him know how very grateful I am."

"I hope it means something," Betty Parker said. "I don't remember his ever saying anything about a root cellar before."

"Keep your fingers crossed," Uncle George said.


The gates at Hilltop were not locked on this fall morning, but Trooper Arbetchian was stationed there.

"Lot of traffic," Arbetchian told Uncle George when he

came around to the side of the Jeep. "Cops, lab technicians, the works. I'm supposed to keep out the curious who have no real business here. I guess you don't fall into that category, George."

"You know if Jake Wilson is on the job?" Uncle George asked. The local man who took care of the grounds for Hopkins would know about a root cellar.

"He's up by the buildings somewhere," Arbetchian said. "Came to work at his usual time, I guess."

Jake wasn't working, however. Like a lot of others he was hanging around, waiting for the State Police to pull a rabbit out of one of their hats.

"Dozens of fingerprints inside Bradshaw's cottage," he told Uncle George. "Most of 'em you'd expect to find." He looked down at his fingers which appeared to be ink-stained. "Mine, Bradshaw's, others they haven't been able to match up yet. What the hell do you suppose someone was looking for in there?"

"I need some help from you, Jake," Uncle George said. "Where is the root cellar?"

Jake looked puzzled. "What root cellar?"

Uncle George told him about old Rich Pettybone. "He seemed to be trying to tell me that Joey could have got into the root cellar, wherever it is."

"There's no root cellar," Jake said.

"Has to be. The old man mentioned it."

Jake shook his head. "I've been working this place for the last three years, every day. There isn't any root cellar, George. Mowed every blade of lawn grass, worked every flower bed."

"Could it be under the house, one of the other out buildings? Place where the Cranes might have stored apples, potatoes, bulbs for spring plantings? They're common enough in this neck of the woods."

"There's a big cellar under the main house," Jake said.

"Nothing under the barns, the garage, the toolsheds or Bradshaw's cottage. I worked on the cottage when it was built—three years ago when Hopkins first hired me. But I never heard anyone talk about a root cellar."

Uncle George reported on how old Rich Pettybone had pointed high up over his head.

Jake laughed. "Root cellar in the sky?"

"I took it to mean somewhere up at the north end of the property."

Jake shook his head. "When Hopkins bought Hilltop he fenced in about fifty acres surrounding the house," Jake said. "Everything inside the fence is cultivated, worked on. I mow the lawn grass right up to the fence, all the way around. There's no root cellar anywhere there, George."

"Abandoned? Not used?"

"No way, no such place."

"Unless it's under the main house—"

The negative head shake was positive. "I've been all through that cellar under the house. Some tools kept there. Sometimes the heating system acts up, or a fuse gets blown. I'm pretty handy, you know. I can handle those small things, or tell the boss he needs an expert. Maybe some closet or storage space was called a 'root cellar' in Rich Pettybone's day."

"What about the north end of the property, beyond the fence?"

"Woods. You know that, George. Goes right along the ridge to the edge of your property. We cut some wood for fireplace burning up there, clean out old dead and dying trees. Why would anyone have a root cellar up there?"

"Hopkins may have old maps, surveys," Uncle George said.

"Could be. I suggest you ask Mrs. Hopkins, though. She's the one who cares about the land, laid out the lawns and the flower beds. The boss doesn't give a damn about

157

that sort of thing. Business with a capital 'B' is his thing. Back and forth to the city in his plane, long-distance phone calls that may add up to more in a month than I make in a year."

"Thanks, Jake. Mrs. Hopkins may be more willing to talk to me than her husband. He thinks I'm trying to harass him."

It wasn't a good day for Delia Hopkins. She was waiting to play out the last act of a painful tragedy. The undertaker was due to bring Anne Hopkins's body back to Hilltop, where it would lie for a day in the room on the second floor before the very private funeral that would follow. Delia was moving restlessly around the big entrance hall, as if she was looking for something lost, when Uncle George found her.

"Oh, Mr. Crowder! Any news of the boy?" she asked.

"No. But I came to ask you for help."

"I—I don't know of any help I can give you, Mr. Crowder. I—I'm waiting here—for Anne." Her voice was unsteady.

"Do you know where a root cellar may be on this property, Mrs. Hopkins?" She gave him a blank look and he went on to tell her about his visit to Rich Pettybone.

"I'm not aware of any such cellar on the property, Mr. Crowder."

"There may have been old maps of the place from the Cranes' day," he said. "Blueprints or surveys when you bought the place?"

"Yes, I have a couple of old maps that were given us when Lucius bought the house. I kept them as a sort of history of the place. I don't know how far back they go. But I can tell you there's nothing suggesting a root cellar on those maps. I studied them pretty carefully when I was planning the landscaping we've done here. Nothing on the surveys either. I'd remember. If there had been such a cellar, I'd have tried to think of something to do with it."

"Could I look at those maps and surveys?"

"If—if you'd come back a little later, Mr. Crowder, I'll try to dig them up for you."

"I'm looking for a lost boy who may be in bad trouble, Mrs. Hopkins."

"I'm waiting for a lost girl, who is—dead," Delia said. He heard a sharp intake of her breath, and she hurried toward the front door.

Looking out through the French windows at the end of the hall, Uncle George saw the undertaker's hearse coming slowly up the winding driveway. Anne was coming home.

Instinct told Uncle George that he had no reason to doubt Jake Wilson or Delia Hopkins. These two people, who knew the property so well, so intimately, would have no reason to deny the existence of old Rich Pettybone's root cellar. It wasn't likely that a search of his own would reveal a place these two people were certain didn't exist. Had old Rich Pettybone been dreaming? Had he mixed up his fading memories of the old Crane place with some other place? Had "root cellar" been a special name, a sort of *in* name, for someplace that wasn't a root cellar at all? Someplace high up, as the old man's struggling gesture had suggested?

He'd just reached his Jeep, not at all certain where to go in it, when he saw Jake Wilson coming toward him, beckoning.

"Stan Boswell, the state homicide dick, is down at the garage," Jake said. "He saw your buggy up here and asked me to find you. They're going over Anne Hopkins's car."

Stan Boswell was standing in the doorway to the garage. Anne's car had been moved to the service area and two troopers were inside it, obviously dusting for fingerprints.

"To add to our collection," Boswell said. He sounded grim.

Uncle George looked at him. "Something else?"

Boswell nodded. "Her keys were on the ignition switch. I opened the trunk. There are bloodstains there, Crowder. A lot of blood. I remembered you'd suggested she might have been killed somewhere else, brought back here by the killer, and dumped in the empty swimming pool. Looks like you may have struck gold."

"Where did it happen?" Uncle George asked himself.

"They've got a car lift here," Boswell said. "As soon as the fingerprint boys are through with the inside we'll hoist her up and see what's on the underside. Nothing on the boy?"

Uncle George told him Rich Pettybone's story and the dead end it had led to.

"Old man's probably badly confused," Boswell said. "If I get there, I hope someone'll shoot me before I start babbling."

The fingerprint men finished presently. "Not much that's any use," one of them reported to Boswell. "Couple of good clear ones on the glove compartment. Probably the girl's."

"Let's hoist her up," Boswell said. He gestured to Martin, the Hopkins's mechanic, who was standing to one side.

It was a simple car lift, used in professional garages to facilitate greasing and underside inspection. The car was lifted and Boswell and Uncle George walked under it.

"Looks like it had been driven through pretty thick weeds," Boswell noted. "Grass stuck to the pan, that right rear brake."

"Hold it!" Uncle George said. "Something's stuck there at the front end."

"So there are weeds."

"Those are wild orchid leaves," Uncle George said. "Scarce in these parts. Take them off easy."

Boswell took the shiny leaves off the inside of the front bumper, and showed them to Uncle George. Uncle George felt his muscles tensing.

160

"Long ago, after I had my trouble," he said to Boswell, "I came back here to build my cabin—start a new life. There was another lost soul around in the woods those days. He'd been a college professor, some kind of botanist. He dammed up a stream in the woods, made himself a little pond. He was interested in plants that grew around water; water lilies, special bulbs and plants, and special variety of orchids. He died a while back, and now these orchids grow wild there."

"Interesting, but so what?" Boswell asked, turning the orchid leaf in his fingers.

"That little pond my friend built is on the back road from the hospital to Hilltop," Uncle George said. "What do you say we have a look?"

For a man with Uncle George's skills the woods told a clearly readable story. There was the place where a car had stopped off to the side of the road; then there were further tire tracks leading into the woods. The two men walked in, careful not to obliterate the tracks. There was the pond, and the place where the car had stopped at its edge.

"You think this was a special place to Anne where she came to think?" Boswell asked.

"Look here at the edge of the pond," Uncle George said. He'd walked a few feet away. "Dog tracks, leading into the water."

"So some animal needed a drink," Boswell said.

"I don't think so," Uncle George said. He was walking along the edge of the pond. "Could have been a dog about the size of my Timmy." He stopped. "Look, Boswell, this is where he came out." The tracks were clearly visible in the muddy edge of the pond. "There was something out there. Joey told him to fetch and the dog went and got it." He stepped down into the water.

"You crazy, going out in that?" Boswell asked.

The little pond was only about ten feet wide and twenty yards long. "It's only a couple of feet deep," Uncle George said. "It wasn't intended for fishing or swimming. Just a place for my old friend to grow his plants."

Boswell watched Uncle George wading out, apparently scuffing at the bottom with his feet. Suddenly Uncle George bent down and reached under the surface with his hands. He straightened up, holding a dripping dark bundle in his hands.

"The girl's clothes," he called out to Boswell. He came ashore and put the bundle down on the grass. He untangled them—the blue slacks, the blue quilted jacket, underpants, shoes and socks. "Weighted down with this rock," Uncle George said, kicking aside a heavy stone.

Boswell showed disbelief. "You trying to tell me your dog could track the scent of the girl underwater?"

Uncle George shook his head. "The shirt's missing. A pink man's shirt she was wearing."

"Will you just tell me how you read it, Crowder," Boswell said.

Uncle George stood looking down at the water-soaked clothes. "The killer stopped Anne on the road, killed her, drove her in here—or maybe the killing was here. Blood all over her clothes. It's washed off now. He stripped her, stuffed her naked body into the trunk of the car. Made a bundle out of the bloodstained clothes, weighted them with that rock and tossed them in the pond. Then he drove the car to Hilltop, garaged it, took the body out of the trunk and threw it into the swimming pool. Got clothes from the house and put them in the bathhouse—"

"Guesswork," Boswell said.

"I don't think so," Uncle George said. "The pink shirt's missing."

"Meaning?"

"I think Joey spotted the car tracks out by the road, followed them here to the pond. Our killer hadn't done too good a job making his bundle of clothes. The shirt came

162

loose and floated to the surface. Joey saw it. The dog wasn't following a trail into the water, Boswell. Joey saw the shirt floating out there, ordered Timmy to go fetch and he did. The boy has the shirt, wherever he is."

"So the killer knew he'd got it—and that's what's happened to the boy," Boswell said. "If the boy had brought it to us we'd have tracked all this down a lot sooner."

"I hope to God you're wrong about that," Uncle George said.


With the press from halfway around the world, TV cameramen waiting for something to keep the news fires burning hot, it seemed important to Boswell to make his case as airtight as possible before any word of it slipped. He wanted plaster casts of the tire tracks by the pond to compare with tires on Anne Hopkins's car; he wanted fingerprints checked against any they already had on record; he wanted an analysis of the bloodstains he'd found in the trunk of the car. The coroner knew what Anne's blood type had been. If the stains in the car were the same type they were on pretty solid ground.

"If those things all check out," Boswell said to Uncle George, "then we won't sound like a couple of gossiping old women when we let people know what we think."

"People?"

The corner of Boswell's mouth twitched. "Bad enough for the girl's mother that her daughter died by accident. To be told that it was cold-blooded murder—" He moved his shoulders as if he could somehow shake off that notion. "Got to tell her and the stepfather. The girl's history takes on a new importance now. There's something we haven't got yet, Crowder. Why did Anne, looking at her boyfriend in the morgue, pretend to you and the sheriff, her friends, that he was a stranger?"

163

"Just a guess," Uncle George said. "She wanted time to think out what she was going to do about information her young man, Comargo, had passed on to her. If she'd confessed to Red Egan and me that she knew who that body in the morgue was, we'd have whisked her off to the State Police, the county attorney; she'd have had to face her parents. She needed time to make some kind of private decision, unmolested."

"Some 'unmolested'!" Boswell said. "Brains beaten in—like Bradshaw, by the way. Stripped of her clothes. Who knows, maybe raped? I want my evidence solidly established before we put the parents and the rest of the household up there on the hot-seat."

Time was beginning to eat away at Uncle George's nerves. It was going on eleven o'clock in the morning. Joey must have left the cabin over the ridge about five o'clock yesterday afternoon—almost eighteen hours ago. If the boy was hurt somewhere it had now been a dangerously long time. If his injury had involved bleeding it was way too long. The night had been cold. But by now many acres of the surrounding woods and valleys had been searched by the men of Lakeview, crossed, and recrossed, and crisscrossed.

Waiting for Boswell to solidify his evidence, Uncle George tried to imagine Joey's pattern the night before. Early evening—out from the road to Hilltop for the hospital; giving Timmy Anne's nightgown to smell. They must have gone up the west side of the road. Joey, trained by Uncle George, had spotted the evidence of a car being driven off the road, followed the tire tracks into the old botanist's pond. Uncle George and Red Egan, searching for Joey later, had worked the east side of the road, missing the tire marks and other evidence that would have led to the pond. The men working the west side hadn't been looking for a car, but for a lost boy, had missed what was there to see in the darkness.

Back to Joey. He had seen and gone into the pond. Timmy, sniffing around, may have shown some excitement. Anne's body must have been there on the grass earlier. Joey, shining his torch out over the pond, must have seen the pink shirt floating on the surface. Uncle George tried to remember if he'd described the clothes that Anne had been wearing to Joey. In any case, the boy had ordered the dog to fetch the floating shirt. The dogs paw prints going into and coming out of the pond suggested that. Of course, Joey could have waded in, snatched the shirt, and not stumbled on the rock-weighted package on the shallow bottom.

What then?

If Uncle George had mentioned the pink shirt to Joey, the boy would instantly have guessed it was Anne's. There could have been a name tag in it. Young people going to school and college often had name tags in their clothes. Timmy, the dog, could have shown some excitement over the shirt. It would have had the same scent as the nightgown that had been used to start him hunting.

If Joey guessed who the shirt belonged to, how would he react? He was a bright, intelligent kid. He'd know there wasn't a body to go with the shirt. Anne's body, taken from the swimming pool at Hilltop, was at the undertaker's establishment in town. Would he have set out to bring the shirt to Uncle George, or would he have decided to take the shirt to Hilltop, turn it over to Anne's family, and tell them how he came to find it? He could have taken the shortcut through the woods that would have brought him to the top of Hilltop's fenced-in grounds. And that could have brought Timmy into contact with the attack boxer who'd later had his throat cut in Bradshaw's cottage. But what of Joey?

He'd had a rifle. Wouldn't he have tried to protect Timmy? If the attack dog was roaming the property, wouldn't Bradshaw have been close by? Bradshaw couldn't answer that question now, but earlier he'd been aware they were searching for Joey and hadn't mentioned a dog fight, or a missing kid.

Back again to the nonexistent root cellar. Where and how? If Joey had found such a place and hidden there, why hadn't he come out now, in daylight, with Hilltop swarming with cops? And how could he come out of a place that didn't exist?

Uncle George was sitting in his Jeep outside the big house at Hilltop when a trooper came over to him.

"Your Homicide friend in New York has been trying to reach you, Mr. Crowder."

"Lieutenant Kreevich?"

The trooper nodded. "Said if we found you we were to have you call him at his office in the city."

"Is there a phone anywhere except in the main house?" Uncle George asked.

"One in Bradshaw's cottage," the trooper said. "I guess Captain Purdy wouldn't mind if you used it. Fingerprint boys are through there."

Uncle George walked over to the cottage, now deserted. He put in a collect call to Kreevich in New York. The lieutenant sounded concerned.

"They told me at the barracks about the boy, George. Any luck yet?"

"No."

"How long has he been missing?"

"More than eighteen hours," Uncle George said. "We've got some pretty solid evidence now that Anne Hopkins was murdered. There are indications that Joey discovered that long before we did. That could mean—" He let it hang there.

"You thought that was murder from the beginning, didn't you, George?"

"It's not much satisfaction to be proved right," Uncle George said. "I don't dare face Esther. She and Hector

166

would be right to blame me—playing detective games with the boy."

"Nonsense," Kreevich said. "Listen, I called you because I have some rather peculiar information about Comargo."

"Anything may be a help," Uncle George said. "The girl knew something she never got to tell anyone."

"What I've got is kind of yes-and-no," Kreevich said. "The Stroud woman told you Lucius Hopkins had gotten Comargo kicked out of college, and then had him fired from two or three jobs. Right?"

"That's what Anne Hopkins told her."

"Well, she was right about the college," Kreevich said. "Do you know what Hopkins told the authorities there? He said he'd caught Comargo trying to steal some valuable art objects."

"So they expelled him?"

"Hopkins had friends on the board of trustees. It was easy enough to persuade them Comargo didn't belong there."

"So Marilyn Stroud was right."

"But after that it doesn't check out," Kreevich said. "The machine-tool place where he got his first job fired Comargo because of orders from the front office. No connection of any kind with Hopkins at all."

"You mean you haven't found a connection yet."

"I mean there is none. I'm certain of it, George. The next place is the same thing. No connection with Hopkins, no connection with the machine-tool people. Orders from higher up."

"Friends of Hopkins?"

"I don't think so. Times are rough, George. People laid off everywhere. 'The last one hired is the first one fired.' That may not be the real reason. But I have to believe there was no connection with Hopkins in the other two places. I've talked to people I have reason to trust."

"Hopkins was after Comargo because he caught him in

bed with his daughter. Got him kicked out of school. You're trying to tell me it is just a coincidence that he got fired from his next two jobs?"

Kreevich hesitated. "I don't say it's coincidence, George. I don't believe in coincidences any more than you do. I do say I'm certain Hopkins wasn't behind the two firings after college."

"Anne thought so because Comargo thought so," Uncle George said. "Comargo, Anne told Marilyn, was coming here because he had something that would get Hopkins 'off his back.'"

"He was wrong if he thought Hopkins had been after him beyond the college thing," Kreevich said.

"Well, I don't know where that gets us, but thanks, anyway, Mark."

"I'll keep digging here," Kreevich said. "The boy's bound to turn up, George."

"I hope you're right," Uncle George said. "I wish I had some confidence left."

_____ 5 _____ Red Egan was standing outside the cottage, smoking a cigarette, when Uncle George emerged.

"They told me you were here, George," Red said. "Didn't want to interrupt your phone call."

"You talked to Boswell?" Uncle George asked.

Red seemed to be trying to avoid looking directly at his friend. "Yeah. Your hunch was right, wasn't it?"

"Everybody says that as though it should make me feel wonderful," Uncle George said. "Well, it doesn't. Joey discovered what had happened yesterday, and he disappears like a whiff of smoke!" He kicked at the ground. "Anyone tell you about old Rich Pettybone's talk about a root cellar?"

Red nodded. "There isn't one as far as anyone knows."

"Mrs. Hopkins has some old maps and surveys. She'll try to find them for me when—when she can."

"I've asked a half-dozen old-timers, George. Nobody's ever heard of one." Red dropped his cigarette and stamped it out. "I've got something to tell you and something to ask you, George. I have to tell you that the search for Joey is winding down. Men have to get back to their jobs, their families. They've covered the woods around here like a tent, George, and there's nothing."

"We've *got* to keep looking!"

"A lot of us will, as long as there's daylight. But after that—" Red made a helpless little gesture with his big, awkward hands. "Boswell just told me that you and he are about to put the facts of life to the Hopkinses."

Uncle George shook his head. "I don't know about Boswell. I'm going to be looking for Joey."

"I think you should be with Boswell," Red said. "I think you should hear what the Hopkinses have to say, see how they react. You're a lawyer, George, practicing or not. You can handle an interrogation better than anyone. You should stay with it. That could turn out to be the best way to look for Joey."

Uncle George didn't answer, staring grimly out across the lawns to the hills beyond the house. He was thinking of old Rich Pettybone's gesture—hand held up over his head suggesting "high up."

"I'd like to go back to that pond and try to find the trail, George. Where did Joey go after he found that shirt?"

"*If* he found it, Red. That's still just a guess."

"So I'll take someone with me and we can make certain," Red said. "I suppose the killer could have disposed of that

169

shirt separately, weighted it down with another rock. If it's there we'll find it."

"Timmy, my dog, went into that pond for something and came back with it," Uncle George said.

"Like you, I think it was the shirt. Boswell's gotten his tire-track molds, his photographs. He won't mind if I mess around down there."

"I'll go with you," Uncle George said.

Red's hand rested on his friend's arm. "You should stay here to hear what the Hopkinses have to tell you. You trust me, don't you, George? I'm not as good as you are in the woods, but I'm good."

Uncle George put his arm around Red's shoulder and for a moment held him close, like an affectionate parent. "I know you're good, Red. I'd trust you with my own life. But Joey's?"

"We've only got human means to find him, George. No witchcraft. I'll give it the best try a man can give. You may get something out of Hopkins that no one else can. That's where you're the best."

"Go, Red. But keep checking back, will you?"

"You know I will. The minute I come up with something I'll come straight to you, no matter where you are."

"Thanks. And, Red, if you pass through town, stop to see Esther, will you? She needs to know we're not giving up."

"I'll get word to her, George, even if I don't see her myself. I promise."

Stan Boswell, the State Police detective, had done an efficient job since he and Uncle George had separated. The plastic molds of the tire tracks they'd found at the pond checked out. They had been made, beyond any doubt, by Anne Hopkins's car. The bloodstains found in the trunk of that car were the same blood type as Anne's.

"RH negative," Boswell told Uncle George. "Rare

enough to make a coincidence seem unlikely. The clothes we found are Anne's, identified by Hilda Clarkson, the maid. Those three things take all the guesswork out of it, Crowder. You ready to give the Hopkinses the bad news?"

"Hopkins isn't going to want me present."

Boswell smiled. "I just made you deputy," he said. "You found the evidence for me. You make it possible for me to prove it out. You are the lawyer for Anne Hopkins and Paul Comargo, aren't you?"

"I have to confess to you that I invented that," Uncle George said.

Boswell's smile tightened. "Remember, I didn't hear what you just said. Let's go."

The big house was curiously quiet when Boswell and Uncle George were admitted into the big entrance hall by Jerry Hopkins. Even that jeering young man seemed unnaturally subdued.

"I think you guys must know that they've brought Anne home," he said, when Boswell had asked to see his parents. "Surely, whatever you have in mind, can wait."

"I'm afraid not," Boswell said. "I need to talk to your parents—and you."

"I'm here, talk," Jerry said.

"I want the whole family present," Boswell said.

"Don't you have any compassion for my stepmother?" Jerry asked. "Annie was her one-and-only."

"If you don't go after them I'll be forced to do it myself," Boswell said.

Jerry produced a twisted smile. "I'll bet you would," he said, but he headed upstairs.

"'Like father, like son,'" Boswell muttered, watching Jerry disappear. "'World is my oyster' department. I wonder what it would be like to feel so sure of yourself?"

"The boy has been brought up to expect nothing less than everything," Uncle George said.

Delia Hopkins was the first of the family to appear. She stood at the top of the stairs for a moment, looking down at them. The dark dress she was wearing accentuated the pallor of her face. She was carrying a sheaf of paper in her left hand, and as she started down she clung, almost desperately it seemed, to the stair rail. Her attention seemed to be focused on Uncle George.

"I rather resent having to deliver these in person, Mr. Crowder," she said. "I have just this last little time with—with Anne. Two recent surveys, one older map. I could have sent them to you by Hilda or Jerry."

"I'm afraid that's not why we're here, Mrs. Hopkins," Boswell said. "Your husband?"

"Lucius had no sleep at all last night, the house swarming with police and God knows who else. He was lying down when Jerry told him you needed him. He'll only be a minute or two."

Uncle George was glancing at the map and the two blueprints of surveys. There was nothing to indicate a root cellar on any of them.

"I could have told you, Mr. Crowder," Delia Hopkins said, noticing his disappointment.

Lucius Hopkins, followed by Jerry, started down from the floor above. Hopkins was wearing a dark blue dressing gown over pajamas, a paler blue scarf tied, ascot fashion, at his neck. Fatigue was written clearly on his face, his eyes almost bright with anger.

"More of the same damned questions, I suppose," he said. "For God's sake, officer, we've told you and your people what we know ten times over. Is there no chance at all that we can be allowed to deal with our personal problems in private?"

"I'm afraid we're not here to ask you for information, but to give you some," Boswell said.

172

"What's Crowder doing here?" Hopkins asked. "He has no official standing that I know of."

"I've deputized him," Boswell said.

"Oh, brother!" Jerry said, from behind his father.

"I think it would be better if we could go somewhere we can sit down," Boswell said. "I'm afraid this isn't going to be quick."

"My study," Hopkins said. "There may still be a fire there." He marched off ahead of them.

Delia Hopkins hesitated, glancing up the stairs toward the room where Anne's body had been taken. "Is my presence absolutely necessary, Mr. Boswell?"

"I'm afraid it is—yours and Jerry's," Boswell said.

Servants had kept the fire going in the study, and the book-lined room had an almost cheerful look to it. Lucius Hopkins had walked over to a far window overlooking the grounds. Delia sat down on the edge of an armchair by her husband's desk, ready to leave the moment she could. Jerry lounged by the door, equally ready for a takeoff.

"I'm afraid what I have to tell you is going to be extremely painful," Boswell said.

"After hours of this bumbling investigation, anything you have to say would be painful," Hopkins said, not turning from the window.

"Thanks to Mr. Crowder's rather special skills," Boswell said, "we now have proof that makes it certain, beyond any question, that your daughter's death was not an accident. She was murdered."

Beyond a little gasping intake of breath from Delia Hopkins, there was a moment of almost complete silence. Hopkins turned slowly back from the window.

"What the hell are you talking about?" he demanded, his voice harsh.

Boswell let them have it, without flourishes; the bloodstains in the trunk of the car, the orchid leaves caught on the underside of it which had led Uncle George to the little pond in the woods, the tire marks there, and the eventual discovery of Anne's clothes.

"Oh, my God!" Delia Hopkins whispered.

"Unfortunately, we are missing a key witness—Bradshaw," Boswell said. "He testified yesterday that he heard Anne come home about four in the morning. That leaves two hours from the time she left Mr. Crowder and Sheriff Egan at the hospital to the time Bradshaw told us he heard her car being driven into the garage. Two hours during which she was waylaid on that mile-and-a-half stretch of road, brutally beaten to death, stripped of her clothes, stuffed into the trunk of the car, and driven back here, where she was thrown, naked, into the empty swimming pool."

"That's just not possible!" Hopkins said, the anger gone from his voice.

"There's one more thing that has to have happened," Boswell said. "At four o'clock in the morning, the killer—or an accomplice—had to have come into this house, gone up to Anne's room on the second floor, selected fresh clothing of hers, and taken them down to the bathhouse. If Mr. Crowder, who is a trained observer, hadn't remembered what Anne was wearing when she left him at the hospital, there might not have been any questions about it."

"She came home, planning to go out again," Jerry said, "changed into something more suitable, decided to stop for a swim, and didn't notice that the pool was empty. All this other crap is meaningless."

"All this other 'crap' is solid evidence, Jerry," Boswell said.

Delia Hopkins was suddenly standing in front of her chair, bent forward like an old woman. "There isn't any chance at all that you're reading this evidence incorrectly, Mr. Boswell?"

"I'm afraid not."

Delia Hopkins straightened up, facing her husband. "Then you're going to have to tell them, Lucius. If you don't, I will."

Hopkins moved toward his desk chair, groping for it like a blind man. He sank down in the chair and for a moment covered his face with his hands.

"You better have your lawyer here, Dad," Jerry warned.

Hopkins waved his arms in a negative gesture. Uncle George found himself reminded of a great, hawklike bird in full flight, struck by a hunter's bullet, and fluttering helplessly to earth. He had never seen a powerhouse of a man so suddenly deflated.

Hopkins looked up at Boswell, and his voice was shaky. "I have been the victim of blackmail for the last three years of my life," he said. "I'm not going to tell you what it is all about, except to tell you that it is something for a separate kind of investigation."

"And yet it has some bearing on what has been going on here in Lakeview?" Boswell asked.

"In a way—yes," Hopkins said. He turned his head from side to side, like a man who didn't believe something he was seeing. "Let me tell you this much. I took an action in my business world some years ago which, if revealed, could have cost my corporation millions of dollars and might have led to criminal charges against me."

"And the blackmailer was—" Boswell asked.

"I haven't the faintest idea, Mr. Boswell," Hopkins said. "I was sent photostats of documents and photographs which made it clear the blackmailers knew something about me that could cost me my business career, and possibly my personal freedom."

175

"You use the plural 'blackmailers,'" Boswell said.

"Periodic demands—and at first they were just for money—were made over the phone. Different voices, obviously more than one person involved."

"You say, 'at first they were just for money.' Later you were asked for other things?"

"A year and a half ago, I was ordered to take another kind of action," Hopkins said. "But let me explain to you how it began. I was sent these photostats and photographs by registered mail—just a little more than three years ago. The sender didn't exist; no such person, no such address. But it was clear that someone had something on me I didn't want made public. Someone had been involved with me in this thing, Joel Bradshaw. He was the son of my best friend, working in Security for my corporation, trusted, and, you could say, a personal intimate. I showed him the photostats and pictures. We knew we were both in trouble, but there was nothing we could do but wait for someone to make a demand." Hopkins took a deep breath. "It came, after about a week. It wasn't for the staggering amount of money we'd expected they'd ask for. It was to be five thousand dollars a month—for the rest of my life! Young Bradshaw and I decided to pay. Bradshaw would, of course, devote himself to finding out who had us on the hook. I—I discussed it with Delia, my wife." He glanced at her. "We had two teenagers to think about, Jerry and Anne. I could afford what was being asked. The alternative was big headlines, a kind of scandalous notoriety that Jerry and Anne would have to live with the rest of their lives. I couldn't undo what I had done. It wasn't a matter of making restitution to someone. So we have lived with it, Joel and Delia and I, for three years. Every month I got a phone call telling me where to deliver the money. There was no way to set a trap for them in advance."

"Different people called to make the demands?"

"Different voices, at any rate," Hopkins said. "If it is one man, he is a consummate actor. Then, a year and a half ago, came an additional demand."

"Having to do with Paul Comargo?" Uncle George asked, speaking for the first time. "It was a year and a half ago that he came here to visit you with Anne."

Hopkins nodded. "Yes. I was ordered to deny Comargo our hospitality, keep him away from Lakeview, and finally, to use my influence to get him expelled from college."

"How could you do that?" Boswell asked.

"I'm a trustee of the college."

"So you accused him of having attempted to steal something from you," Uncle George said.

Hopkins looked surprised. "You've found that out?"

"Lieutenant Kreevich, in New York, just told me a little while ago."

"Did he try to steal something from you?" Boswell asked.

"No," Hopkins said.

"Then why didn't Comargo demand a hearing from the college authorities?" Boswell asked.

"I suspect these people—these blackmailers—had some kind of hold on him, too," Hopkins said.

"But you didn't let up on him, got him fired from other jobs," Boswell said.

"No! The college was the end of it. I was never ordered to take any other action against him. I swear to that, Mr. Boswell."

"Kreevich would believe you," Uncle George said. "He's certain you had nothing to do with the job losses."

"Thank God for that," Hopkins said. "The real facts are bad enough without being charged with something I didn't do."

"But Comargo thought you were responsible," Uncle George said. "He was coming here with information that would get you 'off his back.' I'm inclined to think he may

177

have told Anne what that something was. Which is why she had to be silenced."

"Dear God!" Delia Hopkins whispered.

"But I wasn't on his back!" Hopkins said. "I did just the one thing to injure him. I—I had to!"

"You say Bradshaw had been trying for three years to find some lead to the blackmailers?" Boswell said.

Hopkins nodded. "Backtracking on the affair they were holding over me. He didn't find anything. The contacts with the blackmailers always came to me here, in Lakeview. I persuaded Joel to come here, appear to take a job here at Hilltop, so that he'd be on hand the moment the demand came."

"The blackmailers called you to tell you where to deliver the money each month?"

"Yes."

"Surely a man with Bradshaw's experience could have trapped them when they made a pickup," Boswell said.

"We tried that early on," Hopkins said. "The delivery point was usually a lock box at some airport or railway station. Bradshaw staked out one of those places. They never came to collect the money. Then we were warned that if we tried that again, whoever was sent to trap them would be involved in a fatal accident. We began to be certain we were both watched, which meant more than one person—something we already believed."

"Someone here in Lakeview—or some people here," Uncle George said. "Someone here in Lakeview knew when you left here for the city to make a delivery. They knew if Bradshaw went with you. A simple phone call from here would let a partner in New York know exactly when you left and if you were alone."

"We thought of that," Hopkins said. "We could never come up with a suspect here, or anywhere else."

"And yet this is the place where they operate," Uncle

George said. "Comargo was killed here; Anne was killed here; Bradshaw was killed here."

Boswell turned to Jerry Hopkins, who was standing across the room. The young man looked stunned. "You knew what your father's been up against these last three years?" the detective asked.

"Good God, no! I never heard a whisper of it until just now!" Jerry said.

"Part of the reason for submitting to the blackmailers was to protect Anne and Jerry," Hopkins said. "If Jerry had been told he might have tried something dangerous to help me."

"And Anne was never told?"

"No!"

"You, Mrs. Hopkins, you never told your daughter?" Boswell asked.

Delia shook her head. "There was no reason for her to live her life in a perpetual state of anxiety."

"But you were willing to destroy her happiness by making a phony charge against her young man," Uncle George said.

"We had no choice!" Hopkins said.

Uncle George turned away. "Not if you wanted to save your own hide," he said.

"I didn't live up the advance billing you gave me," Uncle George told Red Egan much later. "The prosecuting attorney with the shrewd skills at interrogation just wasn't on the job."

The ugly story of a man caught out in some kind of crime, submitting to blackmail, eventually forced into false accusations against a total stranger, and in the end, because he let criminals run free, being partly responsible for the death of that stranger, of his own stepdaughter, and, finally, of a young man who had been his friend and ally,

179

should have absorbed and fascinated the man who had once been the county prosecutor.

The problem was that Hopkins's story only served to intensify Uncle George's anxiety for Joey. The people responsible for burying Comargo alive and for brutally beating both Anne and Bradshaw to death wouldn't hesitate to take some sort of violent action against a young boy who got in their way.

Even while Hopkins was telling his story, a gruesome thought had occurred to Uncle George. He and Boswell had tracked down Anne Hopkins's movements on the night she was killed; they had found her clothes weighted down with rocks in the little pond in the woods; they had proved a murder. They hadn't looked for anything else in that pond. They'd proved their case. Listening to Hopkins story, which revealed the existence of a gang of psychotic blackmailers and killers, it occurred to Uncle George that a body could be weighted down and tossed into the shallow pond. The wounded setter had been found not too far from there. Had Joey discovered the truth, been caught at the scene, and destroyed? Suddenly all that mattered was to get back to the pond and make sure.

Uncle George just turned and walked out of the study, out of the house, leaving Boswell to continue the questioning of the Hopkinses. Uncle George drove his Jeep down the back road, the half mile to the pond area. Red Egan had been going to start there in his attempt to pick up Joey's trail. Red's car was parked alongside the road and Uncle George left his Jeep just behind it. But there was no sign of Red when he walked in and stood by the edge of the pond.

The woods were very quiet, except for the occasional call of a bird, warning its friends that someone was intruding on their area. There was the sound of a car passing down the road from which Uncle George had just come.

It *mustn't* be, and yet he had to be sure.

Uncle George walked into the pond and began slowly feeling his way from one end to the other. In some places the water was up to his waist, in others it barely covered his ankles. The old botanist's pool had filled in unevenly over the years.

Back and forth, Uncle George worked his way, feeling with his boots at the bottom, bending down to examine with his hands when he touched some larger obstacle. Each turn across the pond, searching, feeling, he felt his hopes rising. At the center of the pond he straightened up from feeling something at the bottom which turned out to be an old metal washtub. People will throw junk and litter even into a place dedicated to flowers.

Uncle George heard a cough from behind and wheeled around. Standing at the edge of the pond was Norman Perkins, the bearded young reporter for International News.

"This may be the scene of your greatest triumph, Mr. Crowder," Perkins said, smiling his bright smile, "and also of your ultimate defeat."

"A somewhat flowery statement, Mr. Perkins," Uncle George said. Then he froze. It was so unreal that he thought it was some sort of visual illusion at first. Perkins was holding a machine pistol, aimed directly at him. Uncle George's voice was quite steady. "I should have my head examined," he said. "Back in my cabin you watched me handling that piece of paper so carefully, making certain not to leave my prints on it, and yet you never asked me a question about it. You knew what it was."

"Oh, I knew what it was, Mr. Crowder. I stuck it to your door myself."

"You're not a reporter for International, are you?"

"Of course not," Perkins said. "I tried to warn you, but you wouldn't be warned. Now we can't let you go any further."

" 'We'?"

As if it was an actor's cue on stage, two other figures appeared from the bushes behind Perkins. They were Girard and Lawrence, Jerry Hopkins's two friends. They were both armed.

"Enough is enough," Perkins said.

A voice cried out. "George! What the hell's going on here?" It was Red Egan. He had appeared from the hillside behind the pond.

"Just hold it where you are, Sheriff," Perkins said, "or I will cut Mr. Crowder in half for your edification. Ed, he's probably armed. Take care of it."

Girard moved toward the sheriff, gun at the ready.

"Stay cool, Red," Uncle George called out. "It's just possible we can make a deal. Any luck with Joey?"

"You don't have anything to deal with, Mr. Crowder," Perkins said. "You don't have the money or the influence to make you a dealer."

Girard had moved in behind Red Egan and was frisking him, when there was a sharp crack of a rifle being fired.

Perkins screamed, dropped his machine pistol, and fell to his knees clutching a shattered hand. At the same moment Red Egan made a quick move and that startled Girard, who was thrown solidly to the ground. Red had his rifle and aimed it straight at Lawrence, the third man.

"Drop the gun, mister," Red ordered.

And then, out of the woods came a small boy, rifle at the ready.

"You always said to squeeze the trigger gently, Uncle George," Joey Trimble said.

Uncle George came plunging out of the pond and a moment later had the boy in his arms.

"My God, that was great shooting, Dr. Watson," he said, laughing his relief.

\* \* \*

It was many hours later before all the pieces were put together to make one clear picture. Uncle George drove Joey home to Esther and his father, stopping on the way to get help for Red Egan with his prisoners. Red's first move, when he'd been relieved by state troopers, was to go to Hilltop and place Jerry Hopkins under arrest.

Joey's story was the first to be clarified. It came in bits and pieces as a ravenously hungry boy devoured a steak sandwich and glasses of milk served to him by his mother.

The boy had set out to help his beloved uncle, accompanied by Timmy, armed with a rifle, and with the stolen nightgown to give Timmy a scent to follow. They'd arrived at the pond, following the same clues that were to take Uncle George and Boswell there later.

"I forgot to tell you I took a flashlight from your place, too, Uncle George," the boy said. "I found the place where Anne's car had been parked by the pond. Timmy acted real excited, like he'd come on a fresh trail."

"Anne's body had been put down on the ground there," Uncle George said. He was smoking his pipe and sipping a mug of coffee Esther had brought him.

"I flashed my light out over the pond," Joey said. "I saw this piece of cloth floating out there and I told Timmy to go fetch it. He did, and it was a pink shirt with Anne's name on a tag inside the collar. Timmy was very excited, and he kept charging up the hill, barking at me to follow. I did. Timmy was quite a way ahead of me. All of a sudden I heard, like a dog fight. I started to run to help Timmy. I had your rifle, Uncle George. All of a sudden, just outside the fence, the ground gave way under me and I fell. It was a straight drop down, maybe ten or fifteen feet. I—I was sort of stunned. It was pitch dark and I had to crawl around, feeling for the flashlight which I'd dropped when I fell."

"Oh, Joey!" Esther said.

"I finally found the flash and saw I was in some kind of a cave or cellar."

"A root cellar," Uncle George said.

"I don't know," Joey said. "It didn't look like anyone had been in it forever. There was a door at one end, a wooden door, like a cellar door. There was no way to open it. I pounded on it and yelled. Nothing."

"Oh, Joey!"

"There was an old rusty pipe with water dripping from it. I had that, anyway," the boy said. "It seemed like forever when I heard something overhead, from where I'd fallen. And then I heard Red Egan calling to me." Joey's eyes flickered. He was close to exhaustion. "Red lowered his belt down and pulled me out. He was taking me to his car to bring me home when we came to the pond again—and there those guys were, holding a gun on you, Uncle George. I—I squeezed the trigger gently, like you always said."

Red Egan filled in his part of it later. He'd gone to the pond, picked up what he thought might be Joey's trail going up the hill toward Hilltop. He'd reached the fence just outside the Hilltop property when the ground gave way under him.

"Fortunately, the hole through which Joey fell wasn't big enough to take me. My shoulders were too wide to let me fall through. I managed to get out, and then I heard Joey calling. There was a cellar there, maybe fifty, sixty years ago. The hole we fell into, Joey and me, was a kind of long-forgotten ventilator shaft. Rich Pettybone was right, you know. It was a root cellar. The door, which was down below inside the fence, had long ago been planted over and forgotten; long before the Hopkinses, long before any living Cranes. Well, Joey flashed his torch. I saw I could reach him with my belt and I was able to pull him out."

"Boy, was I hungry!" Joey said.

\* \* \*

The next morning, after a long night of questioning the four young men under arrest, Boswell had all or most of it.

"Like always, when you're dealing with a gang," the detective told Uncle George, Red Egan, and Captain Purdy in the trooper captain's office, "somebody cracks. Cooperation may get him a lighter sentence from plea bargaining, or his nerve just cracks. In this case it was the one called Perkins. That is his name, but he isn't a reporter. His father is a rich machine-tool manufacturer. Jerry Hopkins's father is Lucius Hopkins. Girard's father is a shipping magnate. Lawrence's father is in oil. These young men, all in college, got together in a bull session. It turned out each of them had something on his father." Boswell's smile was tight. "'It was going to be my money sooner or later,' Jerry Hopkins told me. 'Why wait?' They joined forces, helping each other, and proceeded to develop solid enough evidence for each to blackmail his old man. Everyone in this world has something he wants to hide. How much will he pay to keep it hidden? The boys were pretty clever at this. They've had their rich fathers over the barrel for three or four years."

"But Comargo? The violence?" Purdy asked.

"Somewhere along the way Paul Comargo, a bright young man but with no financial background, got wind of what was going on. How, I don't know. Maybe they cut him in on a small part of their profits. In any case, he knew things that were dangerous to them. He got really dangerous when he met Anne Hopkins and fell in love with her. Maybe he warned them to leave his girl's old man alone. And then they used their power over their victims to give Comargo the business—Hopkins was forced to get him kicked out of college, Girard's father got him kicked out of the machine-tool job. That's the way it went. Finally Comargo guessed what was happening to him. He loved Anne, he wanted her. He decided to go to Lucius Hopkins and tell him that he was being blackmailed by his own son."

"He told this to Anne Hopkins?" Purdy asked.

"I think he may have, or hinted at it. That's when they went berserk. Comargo not only had to be stopped, he had to be punished."

"Buried alive, for God sake!" Red Egan said.

"Give him time to repent!" Boswell said. "So then Anne found out it was Comargo who'd been murdered, when she saw him in the hopital morgue. I think she chose not to let Crowder and Egan know just then. I think she meant to go to her mother to decide what was the best thing for her to do."

"But she didn't make it," Purdy said.

"She didn't make it because while she was in the hospital looking at the body, Jerry Hopkins, who was watching every move she made, hid himself in her car. When she'd driven a little way toward home he held her up, drove her into the pond, and when she wouldn't listen to reason, he killed her. There was so much blood, he stripped her of her clothes, and stuffed her in the trunk of the car. Tossed the clothes in the pond, as we know, but the shirt came loose. He knew the swimming pool at Hilltop had been drained, and so he took her there and dumped her. Then he went into the house, got clothes, put them in the bathhouse."

"His own sister!" Red Egan said.

"These guys had become violence addicts," Boswell said. "And they weren't through. They were out on the grounds, ostensibly searching for Joey. Bradshaw had separated from them, and they must have been talking together about their problems. Bradshaw heard them, and made the fatal mistake of accusing them, then and there. They were the people he'd been trying to track down for three years. That was his death warrant."

"And then someone searched his cottage, fearing he might have collected some evidence which, in the right— or wrong—hands, depending on your point of view, would lead to them," Uncle George said.

"They would have gone on killing and killing," Boswell said. "You and Egan just got lucky."

Uncle George nodded, smiling a gentle smile. "I taught that Joey so many useless things, according to his father," he said. "The luckiest useless thing I ever taught him was to squeeze the trigger gently." He stood up.

"Going to get some rest, George?" Red Egan asked.

"First I'm going up to the north end of town and tell old Rich Pettybone that he was right about that root cellar," Uncle George said. "It may make him feel better to know we aren't thinking of him as a senile old idiot. And then I have a dog who'll be wanting to come home."

F                          c.2
PEN       Pentecost, Hugh, 1903–
          The copycat killers

| 3-89 | DATE DUE | | |
|---|---|---|---|
| | | | |
| | | | |
| | | | |
| | | | |
| | | | |
| | | | |
| | | | |
| | | | |
| | | | |
| | | | |
| | | | |